BEL NEMETON

Jon Black

BEL NEMETON
An 18thWall Productions book published by
arrangement with Jon Black
verba mea in minibus
desiderium meum
Cover by Barbara Sobczyńska
Design by Elizabeth Duffy Graphics
Text Copyright
Bel Nemeton and all related characters and concepts © Jon Black
Series Edited by Nicole Petit

ISBN-13: 978-1-946033-05-5
ISBN-10: 1-946033-05-7

ALSO BY JON BLACK

FROM 18THWALL

Bel Nemeton

Gabriel's Trumpet (Forthcoming - 2017)

"Bel Nemeton"
          (Featured in *After Avalon*)

"Gabriel's Trumpet"
          (Featured in *Speakeasies and Spiritualists*)

Table of Contents

This is a work of fiction. It draws extensively on the tapestry of human history, language, and mythology for its narrative but also occasionally fudges, tweaks, or ignores facts in service to that narrative. Readers interested in a scholarly examination of the topics presented in this work are invited to consult the suggested sources provided at the end of the book.

Parallels between the legends of Rostam and Cúchulainn are the idea of Dr. Connell Monette, presented in his work, *The Medieval Hero: Christian and Muslim Traditions* (Saarsbruck, 2008).

"Miwnay's Story" is loosely based upon actual sixth century correspondence from the collection known as "The Ancient Sogdian Letters" discovered in 1907 by British Archeologist Sir Aurel Stein. A digitized version of one letter is available, with translation into English, courtesy of the Women in World History curriculum.

Prologue

The dream was over. Tears streaked down his wizened face as he surveyed the landscape. Bodies lie strewn throughout the Camlann Valley. Chill winds carried the stench of smoke and blood into his acute nostrils. He arrived too late, taking too long to escape the bewitching Nimue's imprisonment. His escape was a tale worthy of Arthur and his best knights, but it didn't matter. He had failed in his duty as his king's advisor, wizard, and friend.

In his mind, Myrddin saw how the battle unfolded, as surely as if he had been there. Without the benefit of his counsel and his knowledge of tactics learned from the old Romans, Arthur and his men had simply charged, trusting that valor and strength of arms alone could carry the day against the traitorous Mordred and his Saxon allies.

He envisioned Camelot's finest as they charged the Saxon's fluttering banners along the broad, flat valley. Recent rains swelled the ancient River Cam, threatening to flood its banks. As the king and his company advanced, their formations grew ragtag and discipline frayed. Caring only about being first into the fray, the men ignored the high ground on either side of them. And so they remained ignorant of the surprise Morgana and Mordred concealed there. Myrddin would have done the same had he been in Mordred's place. He shuddered at the thought.

Still, Arthur and his knights had turned the tables, won the battle, and destroyed themselves in the process. Britain's king lingered for several hours afterward, so Myrddin was told. But the old man had not reached the Camlann in time to say goodbye.

He could not believe Arthur was gone. Arthur, whom, as a swaddled infant, Myrddin had cradled in his arms and sang to. Before Uther. Before even Ygrayne. Gone. Now, Brittan was without her king, the foe vanquished, and Mordred no more. Myrddin did not know if Morgana numbered among the living or the dead. He hoped it didn't matter. Without Mordred,

Morgana amounted to nothing. Didn't she? But there would be another wave of Saxons. As far as Myrddin could tell, there would *always* be another wave of Saxons.

"Myrddin."

He looked up, it was Cei. The solemn and sober knight numbered among the handful of Arthur's host not only to survive the battle but remain, mostly, unscathed.

"Is it done?" Myrddin asked, wiping the tears from his face. Cei nodded gravely. Myrddin noticed the wound to the knight's face. His cheek would always have a scar. It would match the one on his heart.

How strange that, at the end, it should come down to the two of them. There had been no love to lose between Myrddin and Cei. Neither made any secret of it. Myrddin found the old warrior tiresome, self-righteous, moralistic, and utterly mirthless. He could only imagine what Cei must think of him. Despite that, each man understood and trusted the other's unconditional love for Arthur. That had been enough to unite them.

Cei surveyed his surroundings, searching. "Bedwyr?"

Myrddin shook his head. "Not yet returned," he clarified, lest Cei should misunderstand him and fear another of their company had fallen. Cei had completed his task, as Myrddin knew he would. He hoped Bedwyr possessed the mettle for what he'd been assigned. The venerable cavalier reminded Myrddin more of a grandfatherly otter than a fearsome Knight of the Round Table. With his gentle voice and kind heart, Bedwyr deserved birth into a better time and place. And yet, they also gifted the knight a curious kind of power. Even dead-hearted Mordred had possessed a soft spot for Bedwyr.

Time moved in circles, Myrddin reflected. It had been the three of them, Cei, Bedwyr, and Myrddin, with Arthur at the beginning. And it was the three of them here, at the end. He had known it would be so. More years ago than Myrddin carried to count or admit, he had dreamed. The kind of dream that Bleys, his ancient mentor, taught him to always pay attention to. In his dream, Camelot burned. Stone. Mortar. The rock foundation itself. Everything consumed in flames.

Camelot burned and it fell to the three of them to dispose of the ashes.

And so they had. His dream had come to pass.

Myrddin studied the knight, "What will you do now?"

Cei considered the question. "Stay here. Rally the others. Try to pick up the pieces. You?"

Myrddin, too, thought before answering. He plumbed the depths of logic and reason as well as his intuition for omens and portents. Though tempted by Cei's answer, he could not allow himself to go there. "Darkness descends upon this land," Myrddin pronounced, "and no man shall stop it. I shall walk the wide world searching for Arthur's spirit. And, if I do not find it, I shall simply go home."

"God be with you in your quest," Cei said.

"And the gods be with you in yours."

Chapter One

"Damn it," Vivian Cuinnsey swore at her computer. Once again the document she was preparing failed to format properly.

"Everything okay, Doc?" Grant, her graduate assistant, poked his head through the door.

"I'll get this. Eventually. It'll be fine."

That stretched the truth. Since becoming department chair last year, she had been immersed in a world of budgets, policies, and academic politics that bordered on vendettas. Keeping a department full of idiosyncratic Celtic Language scholars running was a full time job.

Then there was the graduate seminar she taught. Only one class, but an important one, complete with rubrics, lesson plans, and grading. Vivian thought the move from undergraduate to graduate studies was a bigger transition than going from high school to undergraduate. Both high school and undergraduate revolved around what you knew. Graduate school involved coming to terms with what you didn't know. A little acclimation went a long way in helping new graduate students adjust to that shift.

And, of course, Vivian functioned as her department's chief fundraiser and its public face—to the university's administration, alumni, and the world at large.

Now, she faced additional pressure from an impending meeting with an Irish-American CEO, who, having embraced his roots, was considering a sizable endowment to her department. The document which had frustrated Vivian all afternoon was part of her campaign to make the donation a reality.

Another half-hour resolved the formatting issue. Sending Grant home for the evening, Vivian also prepared to leave. Checking email once more before closing her laptop, she was surprised to find a message from Dr. Weldon Grassley, a venerable professor emeritus with her university's department of archeology. Well past retirement age, Grassley remained on the university's payroll and perpetually in the field at excavations throughout Central Asia.

"Dear Vivian, I found this at an excavation in Uzbekistan. I would be very interested in your thoughts."

The attached photo showed a stele, an upright stone plinth, bearing inscriptions in three alphabets. She did not recognize the top two. The first was all thick shapes and dramatic lines. Thin loops and lines characterized the second. At the bottom, however, Vivian found the familiar Latin script she encountered a thousand times a day, the letters used by English and dozens of other languages.

Though uncertain why Grassley sent the photo to her, it piqued Vivian's interest. Greek inscriptions, courtesy of Alexander the Great, were sometimes found that far east. Latin was another matter entirely. A glance told her that, while the script was Latin, the language it recorded certainly wasn't. That came as no surprise. Many peoples had borrowed the script of the far-reaching Romans for recording languages not previously written. Excluding the cumbersome Ogham script, that included her beloved Celts.

Unraveling the Latin script's phonetics, Vivian saw familiar patterns. They were far better suited to the tongues of long ago Britain, Ireland, and Gaul than to the dusty caravan routes of Central Asia. The inscription seemed to be some form of Insular Celtic, the language family to which all living Celtic languages belonged. The words preserved on the stone stele manifested distinctly Insular Celtic traits like verb-subject-object word order and inflected prepositions. At the same time, they lacked traits associated with the other branch of Celtic, the now extinct Continental Celtic family, such as a third gender form.

Having determined the inscription to be Insular Celtic, Vivian's next task was deciding to which of that family's two sub-branches it belonged. The Brittonic language family, still called "Brythonic" by some older linguists, included modern Breton, Cornish, and Welsh as well as their parent languages and a half-dozen extinct linguistic dead-ends. The Goidelic family of languages included modern Irish, Scottish, and

13

Manx, all of which evolved from Middle Irish.

Dr. Grassley's inscription gave every indication of being Brittonic, specifically the tongue called "Common Brittonic." Between the fifth and seventh centuries, that language held sway from Scotland's River Clyde to France's Brittany Peninsula. After the Romans left Britain, distinct dialects of Common Brittonic began to emerge. Those dialects would one day become the separate languages of Breton, Cornish, and Welsh. Perhaps Cumbrian and Pictish, too. Opinions differed as to whether Cumbrian represented a distinct language or just a dialect of Welsh. And, while everybody had a theory, no one really knew what Pictish was.

Having, at least in broad strokes, placed the inscription's language in time and space, Vivian grabbed pen and notepad. Scanning the weathered letters again, she made a quick translation. Words she thought likely to be proper nouns were put into brackets while she offset confusing or unclear sections with parentheses.

The Great King [Tarkun] (causes to be raised?) this monument. (Unclear) house of the Great Counselor [Mirdin] in his honor. (Unclear) Great Counselor to King [Tarkun] for this (two-ten years?), formerly counselor to Great King [Arturus] of the sunset lands. With Great King [Tarkun's] blessings, [Mirdin] departs to the sunset lands to look upon (its?) green trees and endless water (one last time?).

The inscription was a potential bombshell. A career could be made, or broken, by those few lines in stone. But it might have implications far beyond that. A quick mental calculation told Vivian it was too early to call Uzbekistan. By the time she got home, made dinner, and settled in, it would be the perfect time to catch Dr. Grassley at camp before he left for the dig site.

Leftovers put away and coffee in hand, she sat at her computer. Dart, Vivian's black cat, orbited her legs, occasionally staring up at her with his yellow eyes and big ears. She thought about the scrawny kitten he'd been when he first appeared on her doorstep, one ear inexplicably smudged with motor oil.

Initiating a video chat, Vivian was rewarded with the image of Dr. Grassley's birdlike features, mop of white hair, and thick black-rimmed spectacles. "Dr. Cuinnsey, I thought I might be hearing from you."

"Dr. Grassley, what have you dug up?"

"It is a puzzle, isn't it, my dear? We're excavating near a small structure the locals venerate as the tomb of a Sufi saint. But we've dated it to the sixth century, a couple centuries too old for a Sufi." Grassley paused and cleaned his glasses. "Were you able to translate the Roman script on the stele? Was it Celtic?"

"It was. Common Brittonic, to be exact. And I was, most of it, anyway. I'm emailing the translation now. How did you know it was Celtic?"

"An educated guess. After making a phonetic transcription, I consulted the standard references and did some online research. Celtic was one of the few language families I couldn't rule out. So, I thought I'd see if you could shed any light on this little mystery."

"What are the other languages on the stele?" Vivian asked. "I didn't recognize either script."

"They are both in the Sogdian language," Grassley answered. "The first is the classical Sogdian script. The other is the slightly easier Manichean script. With the caveat that we understand rather less about Sogdian than Celtic, they both give translations broadly matching yours."

That pleased Vivian. Of course, it didn't really answer any questions about the stele or its inscriptions.

"Sogdian is distantly related to modern Farsi," he continued. "The spelling of this word 'Mirdin' on the stele is equivalent to 'Lord of God' or 'Noble of God.' I imagine this would translate conceptually as 'pious leader' or something like that, which sounds like a title. But notice that the word already accompanies the title 'Grand Vizier,' or what you translated as 'Great Counselor.' So, I am inclined to believe 'Mirdin' is a name, not a title."

Grassley flashed a mischievous smile. "Of course,

15

'Mirdin' would also be phonetically identical to the Celtic name of the individual commonly called Merlin, wouldn't it?"

"Careful, Grassley," Vivian shot back with hard-earned caution, "You're about to open one of the biggest cans of worms in Celtic studies. The historicity of Merlin, or Myrddin in Celtic, is very controversial. Even the affirmative camp posits Myrddin is an amalgam of multiple figures stretching across centuries. Arguing for the existence of a single individual analogous to the character from mythology is a good way to end a career."

"An intriguing point, given the reference to the 'Great King Arturus' and the 'sunset lands.'"

Thrilled by those same implications just hours ago, Vivian was suddenly in no mood to discuss them with the elderly archeologist. Again, she cautioned Dr. Grassley about the rabbit hole he was circling.

"You can grasp the momentousness of uncovering Latin inscriptions in Uzbekistan," he told her. "To say nothing of ones used to transliterate Celtic. We're holding a press conference about the discovery next week. I'd really like you to be here in Samarkand for it."

Vivian thought it over carefully. "I'm going to follow this development very closely. But, at this point, I can't justify taking time off from my department based on one find, no matter how unusual."

"Regrettable. I always enjoy seeing you. But I understand. I will keep you informed of any developments."

"One more thing, Grassley."

"Yes?"

"Not a word about the whole Merlin thing. Not one word."

Chapter Two

Her meeting with the CEO went well. If Vivian guessed right, and she usually did, a few more glad-handing sessions would secure the endowment. For now, she shifted to focus to preparing for next week's meeting with the board of regents. Secretly, Vivian dreaded these meetings. She felt like she remained on probation with the silver-hairs who managed her university.

During her first year as chair, Vivian attempted to modify her department's degree plans to make it easier for students to take courses in subjects such as history, anthropology, and sociology, as long as the specific class related to Celtic history, culture, or society. The idea made sense to her. Language, after all, did not occur in a vacuum. And the students seemed to like it. But Vivian drastically underestimated academic territoriality. The chairs of other language departments, fearful they would be forced into making similar changes, banded together to oppose her. Perhaps, in a few years, she would try implementing a more discrete version of those changes. For now, she still licked her wounds.

She had tried to put Grassley's puzzle, with all its bizarre implications, out of her mind. Tried with only limited success. Vivian spent more hours than she cared to admit attempting to date the inscription using telltale elements of its grammar and vocabulary. The latter, especially, suggested that the stele was engraved at a time when Common Brittonic had already fractured into dialects that were in the process of becoming languages. Curiously, the stele included words distinct to more than one of those dialects. That might deserve more attention later. Her working hypothesis was that the inscription's creator had been well traveled and possessed a very idiomatic communication style.

Taking all that into account, in her professional option, the inscription on the stele dated from the mid- to late sixth century. The right era, it had to be acknowledged, for a historical Myrddin. She suspected strongly it had been the native language of whomever composed it. The writing seemed to reflect the organic fluidity of a language acquired from birth rather than the structured precision of one studied formally later in life.

Sitting in her office, writing up follow-up emails to the CEO and his staff, Vivian received another email from Dr. Grassley. "Excavated the structure today. Features are consistent with a dwelling not a tomb. Think you might be interested in the more…unusual…aspects of the interior. Yours, G."

Many photos were attached.

The first one showed a weathered stone building adorned with flowers, colorful scraps of cloth, and bits of paper. This was the structure Grassley referenced during their conversation, Vivian concluded. Using Dr. Grassley and the other people in the photo to provide scale, the building must have been about ten feet wide, a little taller, and maybe twenty feet long.

The remaining photos showed its interior decoration. The spirals and elaborate scrollwork certainly looked Celtic, but that could be coincidence. She knew the Sarmatians and Circassians used similar motifs. It wouldn't be surprising if another steppe culture of the same era, like the Sogdians, did as well.

The frescos were an entirely different matter. The enclosed environment and arid climate combined to create a perfect preservation climate for the paintings, their pigments applied directly to plaster covering the interior walls. Vivid blues of the ocean and greens of endless forests, neither found within a thousand miles of Uzbekistan, testified to that. And were those red deer and otters? One painting could easily be the white cliffs of Dover. The one next to it, the pink cliffs of Brittany. Another fresco could only be Stonehenge. Its trilithons and bluestones, accurately but artistically rendered, rising above Salisbury plain.

It all spoke of a man suffering profound homesickness in a faraway land.

Grassley's photographs of the frescoes concluded with a stylized portrait of a king, painted in the traditional Celtic fashion. The young man, clutching a sword in his hands, was at once both handsome and saintly. Vivian sounded out the Ogham inscription on the weapon's blade, "Caledfwich." That name would become Caliburnus and, still later, Excalibur.

"Grant, send an email to the regents. We need to reschedule the meeting."

"Sure, Doc, why?"

"I'm going to Uzbekistan."

Chapter Three

He had been to the end of the earth, literally. Myrddin found where the sun rose over another endless water. Unless, of course, the Greek sages in Alexandria were correct that men walked on a sphere and all waters eventually flowed together.

There, at the world's end, he traded wisdom at the court of the Sui Emperor, who was said to be immortal. Myrddin had learned secrets there.

He almost stayed. In his wide travels, the imperial court was the most civilized place Myrddin encountered. He spent his days immersed in philosophical discussions, listening to poetry, and games of Go. The court offered simpler pleasures, too, like drinking tea and flying kites.

And there, for only the first or second time since leaving Britain, Myrddin met his equal. The man was a *wu*, a title combining connotations of sorcerer, healer, diviner, shaman, and counselor. Nowhere else had he encountered a term so close to the full meaning of *druid*. In Britain, Myrddin always eschewed the term for himself. He felt himself to be so much more than that one label. But, on the opposite edge of the earth, he could wear it with a warmly-remembered fondness.

The aged wu was a figure worthy of himself, Bleys, or Nimue. As Myrddin had been in Camelot, the wizened old wu served as a minister of state, sage, wizard, and the ruler's personal physician. But, in time, the wu's greed for knowledge proved even greater than Myrddin's own.

Yes, Myrddin had almost stayed. But the palace's civility presented a curse as well as a blessing. The tradition and ritualism of the Sui Emperor's court would frustrate the stodgiest Romano-Briton. Large corners of the world remained unknown to him and so Myrddin resolved to walk toward the sunset once again.

Before departing, he went to the old wu, seeking knowledge of the powerful magic the Sui called "fire medicine" as well as the secret of silk and the elixir of immortality. On the last of those three, the wu refused adamantly, explaining that the secret of immortality was to be used for the emperor alone. The eastern sage drove a hard bargain, Myrddin revealed much arcane lore in exchange for what he sought.

Myrddin departed the imperial court with knowledge of fire medicine and silk. In place of the elixir, the wu told him of the fragrant, mandrake-like root that would not bring immortality but would extend one's life and vigor. Leaving that most easterly of empires, Myrddin's ungrateful camel carried a heavy load of the root.

The Sui wizard had bargained recklessly, proffering knowledge, Myrddin acknowledged to himself, it may not have been the wu's place to give. Myrddin liked the man very much and hoped no harm came to him from the transaction.

Walking westward, Myrddin followed the Path of Silk. He came into a strange land where cities worthy of the Romans sprang from rainless wastes. In these cities were peaceful, honorable people of diverse appearances.

He wondered if, for once, the gods looked favorably upon his prayers. In making this land, it appeared they took two portions of the civilization and refinement of the Sui Emperor's court and added a third part of freewheeling Britain. More than that, here he encountered ghosts of home. Perhaps that was an omen.

In the days when Camelot still stood, there had been a secret language spoken by Palamedes, Priamus, and their kin from the House of Sassanius. Learning of the tongue and deducing it to be unlikely any other of which he knew, Myrddin begged Palamedes to teach him. It took half the knight's life to convince him and more than a few favors besides. Here, Myrddin heard echoes of that speech. Using what Palamedes taught him, and speaking slowly and simply, Myrddin could make himself understood in this new land.

Here were a people paying homage to the spirit world in such a multitude of forms that even Myrrdin found it overwhelming. Some worshiped the God of Rome that was, somehow, also not the God of Rome. Others worshiped one god that was not the God of Rome. In that, too, he found shades of the familiar. Save for their size and opulence, the faith's great Fire Temples reminded him of the simple shrine, with its ever-burning flame, kept by the clan of Palamedes. A third group worshiped no gods and focused on releasing their souls from the cycle of rebirth. Others saw spirits in every rock, tree, and animal. Among this group Myrddin felt most comfortable, able to speak of things unspoken since Britain.

Myrddin found his way to the land's capital and the court of its king. The monarch was young and regal, truly both handsome and beautiful at once. There was no mistaking his strong, agile mind and lively curiosity. Even with his limited understanding of the language, Myrddin saw that Tarkun ruled through reason, not whim or desire.

There was more. Years ago, departing the thrice-accursed valley of Camlann, Myrddin told Cei he would wander the world to find Arthur's spirit. He had dared hope to find it many times before. In Constantinople. At the Sui Emperor's court. And elsewhere besides. Each time, he walked away disappointed. But, if eyes truly were windows to the soul, then the young king now standing before him was Arthur's twin.

Their connection had been instantaneous. Conversing in the tongue of the silk traders, which the king spoke more artfully than he, Myrddin found all his impressions of the young ruler confirmed. Tarkun, in turn, was captivated by the clever, worldly wizard and tales of travel and of service to a great and noble king where the sun sank into the sea. That conversation ended with Myrddin offering his service. And with Tarkun accepting.

Myrddin ceased his traveling and put down roots in the land called Sogdia. It was not Camelot. Tarkun was not Arthur. But both were the closest he had found. And so he stayed. He mastered their strange tongue and curious right-to-left scripts. He served Tarkun just as he had served Arthur before him.

After the tragedy of Camlann and years of self-imposed wandering, having a place he called home soothed him. A land at peace, Sogdia was the closest Myrddin would come to seeing what Britain might have become under Arthur's grandsons, or perhaps, their grandsons…had there been no Saxons. No Mordred. No Morgana. No famine. No Grail Quest.

Of course, such a land brought its own challenges. Where Myrddin frequently had to reign Arthur in, Tarkun was too cautious. The Romans, too, had once known that quandary. How do people keep their virtue intact and spirit strong in a time of peace and plenty? In a time without tests? Myrddin worried. Especially about the horsemen who rode from the north.

For the present, Sogdia came as close to paradise as the gods allowed for humanity. But blaming the gods was sophistry, Myrddin admitted. In truth, human nature blocked the path to paradise without any need for effort by the gods.

Chapter Four

It was the most grueling flight of Vivian's life. First to London, then Dubai, and finally Samarkand. The city's name, she learned from her reading inflight, was itself Sogdian in origin, meaning "town of stone fortifications." She had pushed off most of her departmental commitments for a week. More importantly, Dart was in Grant's care. After all, what were graduate assistants for?

Spending nearly a full day in the air, Vivian reviewed what little was known about the Sogdians. Even knowledge of their kings' names and dates they reigned remained incomplete. Sogdia had been a thriving and affluent trading civilization along the Silk Road. Its peaceable people had been both ethnically and religiously diverse. Animists, Buddhists, Nestorian Christians, and Zoroastrians rubbed shoulders in its climate of tolerance and intellectual exchange.

She also reviewed material infinitely more familiar to her. Almost every word written about Myrddin, whether as a figure of history or mythology, was controversial. And, as she told Grassley a week ago, nothing created more controversy than the question of his actual existence. As best, Myrddin, or Merlin, represented the final link a long chain of historical uncertainties.

If there had been an actual King Arthur, or a historical analog or inspiration for him, he was not to be found in the High Middle Ages of fairytale castles, crusades, and full-body plate armor. Rather, he was a creature from the shadowy semi-history of Britain's Dark Ages, living sometime between the decline of Roman authority and the consolidation of Saxon rule.

It was a world in transition, a time of fire and chaos. Its world of the spirit transitioned as well. Sometimes Christian. Sometimes Pagan. Sometimes seemingly both at once. Precious little was written during the era. And precious little of that survived. Archeology stepped in to fill the gaps. But only slowly, with many holes remaining and available evidence often ambiguous or even contradictory.

After four centuries of conflict, Britain's Celts and its pockets of remaining Roman influence likely put differences aside and stood shoulder to shoulder against the newer, grimmer threat of the Saxons. Perhaps that made Arthur a lingering Roman officer, the scion of Romano-British nobility, or a pureblooded Celtic warlord. All three theories had been advanced.

Whoever Arthur was, he, along with whatever allies could be gathered, had checked the Saxon advance for a generation or more. But, in the end, all his efforts came to nothing. The noblest kind of failure, it offered perfect raw material for epics and romances. That didn't change history's bleak reality. The term "Anglo-Saxon" left no doubt regarding who ultimately won. Except in those remote and rugged pockets where Vivian's Celts hung on. And hung on to this day.

Even had there been an Arthur, or a close approximation of him, that did not guarantee there had been a Myrddin as well. The "wise teacher" represented a universal archetype which could have been attached to Arthur's legend at any point. Hypothetically, and Vivian reminded herself it remained only hypothetically, a "historical" Myrddin could be a patrician Romano-British scholar just as easily as a Celtic Druid. Vivian could not, must not, allow herself to assume the individual mentioned in Grassley's stele was *that* Myrddin. But, whoever he was, the wanderer in Uzbekistan had been no Roman. The Common Brittonic of the inscription proved that.

Even taking for granted Myrddin's Celtic origins, the simple question of whether Arthur's beloved counselor and wizard came from Wales or Brittany provoked academic feuds and bar brawls alike. Thankfully, Vivian's Manx heritage allowed her to remain safely neutral in such rivalries.

Many legends explored Myrddin's fate. Most were fuzzy about what happened the fall of Camelot and his demise. A few stories even claimed he never made it that far, that long before the fall, he so angered Arthur that the king beheaded his counselor in a fit of rage. Afterward, those stories said, Arthur dismembered and burned the wizard's corpse.

The majority of tales, however, agreed Myrddin outlasted his protégé. It was about the only thing they did agree upon…except that Myrddin's weakness for women might have done him in. Or, rather, one woman in particular. Nimue. Some sources said she was a Northumberland princess. Others, a "huntress," which, certain scholars alleged, had been the medieval patriarchy's euphemism for a priestess of one of the Celt's fierce nature goddesses. Some identified her as the half-fey Lady of the Lake. For others, Nimue was, like Myrddin himself, a powerful wizard in her own right.

Most sources said Myrddin became smitten by Nimue. Eventually, she imprisoned Myrddin. In a cave. A standing stone. A magical tower. Or even a tree. Her alleged motivations were even more numerous than his alleged places of imprisonment. Disgust at his base obsession with her. Her own desire to possess him. Fear of his power. Greed for his knowledge. Using him as a pawn in her vendetta against Bleys. Preventing Myrddin from aiding Arthur. Imprisoned, Myrrdin either died or remained in a kind of magical stasis. Perhaps to this very day, if you believed in such things.

France's Paimpont Forest, long ago known as Broceliande, contained an alleged tomb of Myrrdin, complete with standing stones. Most scholars, however, did not take the site seriously.

A few sources claimed the wizard did not die in the traditional sense, but simply left the world. By climbing Yggdrasil, the world tree, or ascending from Bel Nemeton, the sacred grove of the god Bel, transcending worldly concerns and never returning. A Breton legend said Merlin climbed a sacred pine tree to the heavens, where he received a mystical revelation so profound that he never again returned to earth. An alternate version placed the pine tree in Glastonbury, even claiming the location took its name from the event: *Glass* for "green" and *tann* for "sacred tree."

Those covered only the common tales. Dig deeply enough, Vivian sighed, and you would find an almost endless supply of outliers, from the intriguing to the crackpot. Too bad that, even allegorically, none of the stories seemed to suggest Myrddin wandered thousands of miles into Asia's heart. True, the *Livre d'Artus* said Myrddin had gone to Rome, entering the Eternal City on the back of a giant stag in order to interpret a dream for the emperor. Of course, the *Livre d'Artus* also claimed the emperor in question was Julius Caesar, whose assassination occurred half a millennium before the birth of the man she sought. So that account should be taken with a grain of salt. She knew all of them should.

She renewed her resolve to stay gun-shy when discussing Myrddin with others. In the privacy of her own head, however, Vivian realized she was becoming less so.

From the air, Samarkand appeared to be a place apart; a separate creation by some god whose first love was desolation. A few unremarkable glass and steel skyscrapers gave halfhearted testimony to the outside world's existence. With its turquoise-capped mosques and gracefully arched structures of stone and baked clay, the rest of Samarkand looked much as it must have in the days of the Silk Road. A tiny swath of green encircled the city. Beyond, rocky desert stretched unbroken in all directions.

Clearing passport control, Vivian was greeted by Dr. Grassley's welcoming grin. His gangly arms wrapped her in an affectionate hug before introducing his colleagues from the excavation's partner institutions. Dr. Laziza Abdulin, from Samarkand State University, was a petite woman in her late-twenties. Dressed in a tasteful pantsuit and matching hijab, she radiated energy. She was quiet, with the eyes of someone who misses little and leaves much unsaid. Dr. Adrian Price, from the School of Oriental and African Studies in London, was near Vivian's age and maintained a reserved air of patrician elegance.

Nothing had prepared Vivian for Samarkand's streets. Bumper to bumper, the motley assortment of European sports cars, four-wheel drives, aging Ladas, ancient buses, and donkey carts had one thing in common. They were all going nowhere fast. Only the flocks of mopeds and bicycles, darting

27

like hummingbirds amidst elephants, moved.

After checking-in to her hotel, one of those lonely modern buildings she had glimpsed from the air, the archeologists treated Vivian to dinner in the city's old quarter. One thing could certainly be said for the Uzbeks, they knew how to eat. Platters of spiced minced lamb, roasted beef, hot flatbread, and rice with apricots and nuts left her feeling fit to burst. As the quartet dined, they discussed the upcoming press conference. The three archeologists dropped hints of some big announcement but all of them, even Grassley, remained coy about specifics.

They also talked about the dig itself. While a certain amount of theft and smuggling was expected at excavations in remote parts of the world, the problem as this site had proved endemic. The archeologists suspected a mole somewhere on the dig crew.

Detecting a faint musical lilt in his otherwise flawless Oxbridge accent, Vivian inquired about Dr. Price's origins. The archeologist, it turned out, was Welsh and from an old Swansea family. Occasionally speaking with him in the tongue of his native land, Vivian felt she softened his aloof exterior just a bit.

Before separating for the evening, Grassley caught her alone. "I have something for you, my dear."

"You're going to let me in on the surprise that the three of you keep hinting about?"

Grassley laughed, "Even better." Reaching into his pocket, he pulled out a small bracelet of delicately worked bronze. "We found this in the structure," he beamed. "The preliminary processing and necessary paperwork is all done. When you get home, I'm sure my colleagues in the archeology department will find it a worthy addition to our collection. Until then, consider it a gift."

Back at her hotel, Vivian examined the bracelet. She was no archeologist, but she knew enough to recognize a combination of Celtic and Roman styles in the elegantly crafted piece. Aware that it was most unprofessional, she slipped it onto her wrist. It fit perfectly.

Chapter Five

In the open courtyard of Tarkun's place, Myrddin watched the king's eldest son, a youth on the threshold of manhood, receive armor, a stout bow, a shining scimitar, and a fast horse. The items physically embodied the martial virtues expected of a prince. He was then presented a gilded staff, silk shawl, and a small chest of gold coins. The gifts symbolized, respectively, leadership, wisdom, and prosperity.

Since time immemorial, this had been Sogdia's ceremony for welcoming a royal prince to manhood. For the first time in memory, an addition had been made to the ritual. Walking forward, resplendent in his silk-robed finery, Myrddin placed a golden torc around the younger Tarkun's neck. That act had been the heart of the coming of age ceremony in Myrddin's homeland.

"Thank you, my grandfather," the younger Tarkun whispered in Brittonic. It was the secret tongue of Palamedes and his house that gave Myrddin the idea of teaching Brittonic to Tarkun, his family, and his best knights and officials. It allowed them to communicate among themselves without being understood by others. Most of them learned only as much as they needed. The younger Tarkun had taken to the language like a fish to water. Were he suddenly transported to Britain, the young man would have no problem being understood.

And, if the younger Tarkun's spirit did not burn quite as brightly as his father's, he was even steadier and more steadfast. Good hands would hold Sogdia for another generation. Myrddin suspected the younger Tarkun's child would be a strong, just ruler as well. Beyond that, no mortal could truly say.

The elder Tarkun, King of Sogdia, placed a gold circlet upon his son's head. Then, with blessings on the young prince from representatives of Sogdia's four great faiths, the ceremony concluded. The younger Tarkun was welcomed to his manhood and royal princedom.

Following the ceremony, Myrddin returned to the place he called home since arriving in this land. King Tarkun wanted him to live in the palace. But the old stone house just beyond the capital's walls gave Myrddin the solitude he craved while also keeping him connected with nature, even in the shadow of a great metropolis. It served another function as well. It went too far to say that familiarity bred contempt, Myrddin reflected, but it did create complacency. His singular residence allowed him to preserve the sense of mystery, of otherness, essential for being an effective counselor and mentor.

He had painted its interior walls with familiar faces and images of home. Curios from his years of wandering as well as fond reminders of Britain adorned it. Pride of place belonged to the bracelet. It was nothing, really. Just a little bronze trinket. Still, it had been Nimue's. It was all he had to remember her by. He supposed he should be bitter. Somewhere, he could almost hear the ghost of Bleys saying "I told you so." Maybe bitterness lived in Myrddin's mind. In his heart? Never.

By Myrddin's reckoning, he had witnessed nearly 100 turnings of the year. It was a potent number in any culture. He thought briefly of the clever counting system he learned from the sages of the Deccan Plateau. In his mind, he saw the "1" slide into place in a new column, followed by two of those ingenious placeholder digits which carried meaning but no value.

Even had all the stories whispered by Britons about Myrddin's origins been true, he could not have much time left. True, no Arthur remained to return to. No Camelot. But he still yearned to hear the laughing waves and smell the fragrant pines one more time.

Perhaps it was Bleys who, long ago, put the idea in his head. As the two of them conversed in Bleys' cave, his mentor suddenly looked past Myrddin, staring out of its solitary entrance. "Sleep is never more restful than in your homeland," Bleys said. Myrddin wondered if he imagined his mentor's wistfulness as Bleys gazed northward, "All the more so for the great sleep which all must someday take." Bleys, he knew, was audacious enough to have a plan to avoid the great sleep. But also realistic enough to know even he would be unlikely to succeed.

With his great sleep nearing, Myrddin's bones cried out to slumber in their native soil. Home was calling him. He resolved to go.

Chapter Six

The following morning, the three archeologists picked Vivian up at her hotel in a minivan. The idea of showing her around their excavation, an hour and half south of Samarkand, had been Grassley's idea. No doubt much remained to be done before the press conference. But, as repayment for help in deciphering the stele, Grassley insisted upon giving her a personal tour.

She didn't know how Drs. Abdulin and Price felt about that. But, by now, they had no doubt learned, as she had, it was sometimes easier to indulge Dr. Grassley's professional enthusiasms than fight them.

Living conditions for archeologists in the field had improved dramatically since the discipline's wild and wooly days of the nineteenth and early twentieth centuries. Nevertheless, no one would call their camp luxurious. Not for the first time, she marveled that the septuagenarian Grassley bore his chosen lifestyle so well.

Vivian's personal tour began with the main excavation site, a fortified palace and settlement once known as Kafir Kala. To its north, the Sogdians had constructed an extensive cistern and elaborate irrigation system. Grassley, however, was unable to contain his excitement and quickly dragged Vivian and the others toward a solitary stone building half a mile east of Kafir Kala.

Vivian, of course, had seen it in the photos he sent. The structure felt smaller than in the pictures, almost lost amid the arid, rocky landscape and the vast blue sky above it. Yet its isolation, and the obvious reverence shown for it by the local population, lent the building a gravitas out of all proportion to its size.

As they stood outside, evidence of excavation abounded. Wooden stakes and twine divided the ground into grid squares. A table sifter stood nearby. Its wooden-framed mesh screen sifted every ounce of dirt excavated, ensuring no artifact, however miniscule, remained undiscovered.

"We're rushing to complete excavation of the structure. Not nearly as thoroughly as I'd like," Grassley admitted. "Even though dating clearly shows this structure is not the tomb of a Sufi, locals' opinions appear little changed." Vivian was not certain, but thought the venerable archeologist might have given Dr. Abdulin a pointed glance as he spoke.

"Of course," Dr. Abdulin added, equally pointedly, "that would not preclude the site from being repurposed and a Sufi from residing or being interred here at a later date."

"There's just no evidence of it," Grassley continued, "Surely, you must acknowledge…"

"What remains to be done?" Vivian interjected, motivated at least as much by desire to forestall an argument between the archeologists as by genuine curiosity.

"We're wrapping up excavation inside the structure. Only one major task remains. Let me show you. I would be interested in your feedback."

Vivian accompanied the three archeologists inside the dwelling. It was a sentimental fallacy, but standing inside, she imagined breathing the same air as its long ago occupant. The floor, she noted, had been excavated already. There, she knew, Grassley had found the bracelet Vivian now wore. The frescoes quickly drew her gaze, the paintings even brighter and more mysterious in real life than they looked in the photos.

She suppressed an urge to reach out for them. Short of taking a baseball bat to the frescoes, something she couldn't conceive anyone in their right mind doing, touching them was the worst thing she could have done. Salts and oils on human skin were devastating to ancient pigments. Nevertheless, Vivian yearned to run her fingers across them. To make a physical connection with that long ago world.

"Look carefully at the frescos, now," Grassley said. "Do you see anything amiss?"

She counted seven frescoes. Two on each wall…except for the eastern wall. It sported only a single painting, the portrait of the young Celtic king cradling history's most famous sword. The regal fresco was not centered on the wall, Vivian noted, but offset to the right instead.

"There's space for an eighth fresco," she observed.

"Is there?" Grassley baited her, "Look more closely."

Scrutinizing the left half of the wall, something was different about it. The plaster was slightly grayer in color. As if added at a different time. Perhaps with a slightly different composition. Reading Vivian's expression, the elderly archeologist nodded with satisfaction, "That's right. Something's been covered over."

As they spoke, a woman wearing overalls, a dust mask, and safety goggles entered the structure, a large metal toolbox at her side. Spotting Vivian, the new arrival spoke, muffled by the dusk mask. "Dr. Cuinnsey," though the mask hid her mouth, Vivian heard the smile as she spoke, "Good to see you. Dr. Grassley said you'd be visiting us."

Cherise Barkley was one of the most valued members of the archeology department at Vivian's university. While well-deserved, it constituted a welcome surprise in academia's status-conscious world. For all her expertise, Cherise lacked a doctorate. Instead, she spent her life questing after an endless series of master's degrees. Archeology. Art History. Chemistry. History. Vivian didn't know what else. Cherise's versatility made her an incredible asset for the department, especially when uncovering and preserving art instillations at remote excavation sites.

"Cherise, good to see you, too. What are we doing today?"

"A little bit of surgery," Cherise said as she opened the toolbox, revealing a collection of odd and esoteric implements. Apparently, she was not kidding about surgery. Removing a scalpel from her box, Cherise began gingerly and methodically scraping the discolored plaster away from the wall. The appearance of a tiny patch of robin's egg blue beneath the off-white surface rewarded her efforts.

Standing over the conservator's shoulder, Vivian became engrossed in the painstakingly slow process. Cherise's delicate, deliberate movements were hypnotic. Almost meditative. And there was the incrementally growing gratification provided by the expanding pallet of blue, gray, white, black, green, and, eventually, red revealing themselves underneath the plaster as she continued.

At last, Cherise stepped back to survey her handiwork. Seen for the first time in centuries, the eighth fresco was another portrait. Vivian leaned in for a closer look. Clutching a vividly red apple, a woman stood in front of a Celtic stone tower atop a green hill. A blue pond or lake stood to one side of the hill. Something in the figure's aspect gave Vivian the impression of a woman on the cusp of middle age, but with few telltale signs of aging. With her fey features, long black hair, and fierce gray eyes, she remained striking.

"If Myrddin, or someone like him, really lived here," Vivian indulged the idea as she rhetorically interrogated the fresco, "who does that make you, dear?" On a wall next to Arthur, Gwynhumara, more commonly known as Guinevere, represented the obvious choice. It was also incorrect. That Vivian could not explain her certainty the woman was not Guinevere did not dilute the strength of that conviction. But who, then? "Ygrayne? Morgan? Nimue? Some saucy bit lost to history?"

The other archeologists stared. Whether because she was talking to a painting or for some other reason, Vivian couldn't quite work out.

"Why ever would this be covered up?" Grassley asked.

"If a holy man lived here later," Vivian ventured, "He might not want the temptation of a sixth century pinup." Her observation earned an approving nod from Dr. Abdulin.

Vivian was glad Grassley had rushed her through the first part of the tour. Being present to see Cherise uncover the eighth fresco had been more than worth it.

Chapter Seven

Dinner at camp lacked the elaboraten preparation of her meal in Samarkand the previous evening. But it was warm, spicy, and filling. Again, Vivian found the conversation fascinating, a window into a different world. Intensive fieldwork brought research difficulties and logistical challenges making for interesting stories. While Vivian's research sometimes involved travel to dusty institutions in remote corners of the world, the lion's share of it still occurred on her laptop or at her office desk.

Pouring tea for his colleagues and their guest, Dr. Grassley turned to Vivian. "My dear, you've given us the benefit of your knowledge of the Celts. Tonight, I thought it only fair if we entertain you with our knowledge of the Sogdians," he explained.

"I've picked out a little story I think might be of interest to you. A story from the life of the hero, Rostam," Grassley said. "Today, Rostam is best known from Persian mythology. But he can be found in the myths of civilizations throughout Central Asia. Some of the most elaborate Sogdian murals ever discovered depict his deeds. The most famous part of his myth cycle is the *Haft-Khan e-Rostam*, the Seven Labors of Rostam."

The archeologist began his tale. In Rostam's first labor, the hero's horse had been gravely wounded while defending his sleeping master from a hungry lion. Awaking, the grateful Rostam healed his steed. The second labor began with Rostam traversing an endless desert, dying of thirst. Praying for deliverance, the hero's piety was rewarded by the appearance of a sheep which led him to a fountain. The third labor told of Rostam's fight with a crafty serpent that, of course, the hero vanquished. The fourth labor represented nearly a full tale in itself. Rostam discovered a lush and fertile land where all things were available without toil and where he encountered a beautiful sorceress. Giving a prayer of thanks, Rostam's holy words revealed the land to be only an illusion and the sorceress a demon, whom he quickly dispatched. In his fifth labor, Rostam defeated the warrior Olad, the champion of Rostam's enemies. For the sixth labor, Rostam rescued Kauui Usan, a mythical Persian King who legend said reigned for 150 years and traveled on a magical flying throne carried by enchanted eagles. When the throne crashed in a land of demons, Rostam had to rescue the king. In his final labor, as he helped Kauui Usan escape, Rostam slew the Demon King.

In Rostam's labors, Vivian recognized obvious parallels with the Twelve Labors of Hercules. While acknowledging the universality of myth patterns, she also knew Central Asians could have heard stories of Hercules during Alexander the Great's campaigns. But there were significant differences. While most of the Grecian demigod's tasks had been simple feats of strength, many of Rostam's labors amounted to tests of virtue. Another set of parallels, however, intrigued her even more.

Grassley beat her to the punch. "Our guest may notice similarities with the legend of Cúchulainn, the great hero of Irish mythology," he teased. "It raises an interesting question about whether the Central Asians could have heard tales of Cúchulainn from someone. And, if so, whom?" As Dr. Price choked on a mouthful of tea, Vivian, like Rostam's vanquished lion, bared her teeth in warning to her elderly colleague.

Feigning ignorance of his transgression, Grassley shifted focus, "Perhaps one of my colleagues has a Sogdian story more to your liking?"

Smiling, Dr. Abdulin rested her teacup beside her. "This is the story of the tribulations of Miwnay, a pious Mazdayasna woman, that is to say a Zoroastrian, of Sogdia," she began. "Miwnay married a man, a trader with big dreams, who moved them to the Sogdian quarter of Dunhuang, a Silk Road city on China's western frontier during the time of the Sui Dynasty. When the trader's dreams did not prosper, he showed himself to be not a man but a pig on two legs. To keep himself from falling into poverty, he renounced and abandoned Miwnay."

Vivian knew nothing of Dr. Abdulin's background. But, somewhere, the archeologist had learned the traditions of oral storytelling and epic poetry. Getting comfortable in her camp chair, Vivian settled in to enjoy the performance.

"Though circumstances reduced her to begging," Dr. Abdulin continued, "misfortune did not cause her to lose faith or stray from the commandments of the *Avesta*, the Zoroastrian's holy book.

"She went to the husband that abandoned her, pleading with him to send her home to Sogdia. Again, the beast renounced her. And still Miwnay did not lose faith or stray from the commandments of the *Avesta*.

"She wrote to her mother, asking for help in returning home. Many weeks she waited for a reply. When it came, her mother said the family's poverty meant they had no help to give. Still Miwnay did not lose faith or stray from the commandments of the *Avesta*.

"She wrote to the mother of the husband that abandoned her, pleading for the support in returning home that the woman's son should have provided. Many weeks she waited for a reply. When it came, the mother-in-law said that if Miwnay's family would not help her, her former husband's family could be expected to do no more. Even then, Miwnay did not lose faith or stray from the commandments of the *Avesta*.

"At last, she went to the Magi, the Zoroastrian priest, in Dunhuang to plead for help. When she finished her tale of woe, the Magi said to her, "Daughter, through everything you endured, you did not lose faith or stray from the commandments of the *Avesta*. I shall give you a camel, a trustworthy man to escort you, and you shall return home.

"So it was that Miwnay returned to her home and family, living out her days in peace and piety."

Vivian applauded enthusiastically.

Dr. Price, who had recovered from swallowing a mouthful of hot tea down the wrong pipe, spoke next. "I suppose it is my turn now. Dr. Abdulin's story gave me an idea. As I think you know by now, Sogdia was a land built on trade and maintained by diplomacy. The Sogdians excelled at both. While probably preferring trade and diplomacy to military expansion, their neighbors were often ambivalent about the Sogdians. The Chinese, in fact, had a proverb that, at a Sogdian's birth, his parents dripped honey in his mouth and stuck resin to his palms. That way, his words would always sound sweet and coins would always stick in his hands."

Vivian gave a cynical bark of laughter. History was not always encouraging. Humanity's ugliest traits, ethnic stereotyping for example, had long pedigrees indeed.

As their conversation became increasingly punctuated with yawns, the four turned in for the night. While most of the excavation's diggers and other local workers slept in large canvas tents, the supervisors and archeologists lived in small aluminum trailers. Onsite was an extra trailer for important visitors like Vivian.

The trailer had corrugated metal sides, two oval windows, and a single wall-mounted air conditioning unit. Though she was currently its only occupant, two Spartan bunkbeds allowed the trailer to sleep four. A desk, small dresser, metal sink with a tiny mirror, and composting toilet rounded out the amenities.

"Ah, the glamor," Vivian said, reclining on the bunk and closing her eyes.

Sleep came, when it came at all, in fits and starts. Perhaps jetlag was finally taking hold. Vivian cursed. Eventually, she quit fighting. Getting out of bed, she splashed water on her face, dressed, and left the trailer.

A handful of local dig workers huddled around a camp stove, drinking tea and shouting excitedly as they gambled with dice. Her sudden appearance surprised them, but they nodded congenially before returning to their game. A gentle yet steady breeze blew from the west and the desert air had grown mild, almost cool. Briefly, Vivian considered returning to the trailer for her jacket. Instead, she elected to continue.

The lights of camp fading away, Vivian noted the sky's vivid midnight blue. The Milky Way, a faint but visible band, stretched across the heavens. Vivian was dimly aware her steps took her toward to the strange dwelling around which this entire affair revolved.

The ancient building was an inky-black silhouette against the outsized full moon rising slowly into the sky. Circling around, Vivian found the other side bathed in moonlight, the stone house appearing luminous. Cloth prayer flags attached in veneration by locals to the house and nearby trees fluttered in the wind.

She contemplated the structure. A millennia and a half ago, something unusual, perhaps even extraordinary, had occurred here. But what? Who, really, was the man that lived here? And how did it connect with the body of lore she spent her life mastering?

Her reverie was disturbed by awareness that Dr. Price stood nearby, no more than a dozen feet from her. Either he had been here already, all but invisible, or he had approached with the quietude of a cat. Vivian thought briefly of the stories of the *Sleih Beggey*, the little people, her governess told her as a girl when visiting relatives on the Isle of Man. To the fey was credited such preternatural stealth.

"*Noswaith dda,*" Vivian greeted Price with a "good evening" in the tongue of his native land.

He replied in kind, a distance in his voice. She studied the man, with his shock of thick, glossy black hair and long, graceful artist's hands. Like the building in front of them, Price's pale-olive complexion appeared luminous by moonlight.

He, too, appeared lost in contemplation. Whether of the structure or something else, Vivian had no notion. Breaking the silence, Price again spoke in Welsh. "Few places are as ancient as Central Asia. Yet, for all that, its archeology and history remain terra incognita to the outside world. But there are secrets here. Deep secrets for those who can find and interpret them."

Vivian had wondered how the Welshman came to select Central Asia as his life's work. His remark suggested that the subject had a nearly mystical hold over him. That did not surprise her. Many scholars felt that way about their chosen focus. His remark told her something else. Price's Welsh was more than passible. Both elegant and poetic, it was better than hers.

"It sounds like you could have translated the Celtic inscription on the stele yourself," she complimented.

"I could have. And did. But Grassley insisted upon you." Though his tone was civil, it held an unmistakable reproach.

Vivian flinched but resisted the urge to apologize. Science depended on its forms and procedures being observed. Whatever Price's personal proficiency, making translations of the stele's inscriptions academically valid required a credentialed Celtic language scholar. Like Vivian. More than that, his dig was uncalled for.

What followed was even more so. "Don't fool yourself into thinking you can master a lifetime of lore," Price proclaimed, "or lifetimes, in only days or weeks. You are an interloper. It is dangerous to be an interloper here."

If that was the warning it appeared to be, what did Price mean? Or could it be it some kind of threat? Surely not, Vivian thought. The archeologist was as eccentric as he was enigmatic.

Perhaps sensing he crossed a boundary, Price continued "Not that I fault your participation or your translation." As an afterthought, he added, "it took me awhile to work through the inscription's archaic consonant mutations and imperfectives." Without directly acknowledging it, he implied Vivian had done it better, or at least faster, than he had.

It approximated an apology, she supposed. Nevertheless, the exchange, and the man's undeniable presence, shattered her contemplative mood. Suspecting she would not regain it tonight, Vivian excused herself. Back in the trailer, to her surprise, sleep came easily.

Chapter Eight

After a predawn breakfast, the four returned to Samarkand. The archeologists needed the morning to prepare for the press conference. That suited Vivian. Back at her hotel, Vivian enjoyed a long soak in the tub and, still fighting the effects of jetlag, took a two hour nap. Rising, she caught up on professional email, trying to keep her little departmental kingdom from falling apart without her.

A friendly email from the CEO reconfirmed her instincts that the endowment would soon become a reality. Grant sent photos of Dart clowning on bookshelves. While neither the best nor the worst graduate assistant she'd seen, Grant understood how to keep the boss happy. The printer on the third floor was acting up again, with one of the administrative assistants threatening to go "Office Space" on it. On a more serious note, Dr. Knox accused two junior-level students of plagiarism. Unfortunately, it looked like at least one of those cases had legs. Vivian knew she had a reputation among the students for being a "softie." Her reputation did not extend to this matter. On plagiarism, Vivian was soft and yielding as steel.

For the convenience of the foreign press and international academics which the archeologists hoped to attract, the press conference was being held at one of Samarkand's chic, modern downtown hotels. Unfortunately, not the one where Vivian stayed. After a light lunch, a hotel chauffer drove her to the conference.

Vivian was greeted immediately by Dr. Grassley who took obvious pleasure escorting her to a first row seat. At the front of the room, a raised platform with three empty chairs and a microphone indicated where Drs. Grassley, Abdulin, and Price would sit. More intriguing was the small display table in front of their chairs. A black cloth covered the table, concealing a lumpy form beneath.

As Vivian moved to examine the table and its mysteriously concealed object, Grassley intercepted her. The archeologist wagged his finger and gave her a grandfatherly "tut-tut." She supposed she could wait a little bit longer.

It pleased Vivian that the conference room was so full. She spotted many of her colleagues from around the world, specialists in the languages, history, or archeology of the Celts. Though she wouldn't recognize them, she knew their counterparts specializing in Central Asia were here as well. More surprisingly, plenty of journalists had come. TV crews with their frenetic "hurry up and wait" energy, bloggers and electronic media journalists on a mission, scruffy radio reporters blessed and cursed that nobody knew what they looked like, and print journalists clutching their notepads like noble relics of a bygone era.

Between the academics and the journalists sat several questionable-looking individuals Vivian couldn't place. "Who are they?"

"Vultures," Grassley responded. "Treasure hunters. You get used to their type working out here." The archeologist identified some of the more infamous ones for her. "That's Mikhail Levich," he discreetly pointed at an avuncular man wearing a finely tailored suit and a Rolex. "He was with the KGB in Uzbekistan back when it was part of the Soviet Union. He still has a lot of influence." Next, Grassley indicated a man in a cowboy hat. "That's Jake Booker. He founded a company making a lot of money prospecting for oil and gas. Then he went into treasure hunting." Finally, he gestured to a small man in an extravagant uniform and wearing mirror shades. "That's Gumanizov. He's a general in the Uzbek army. But his real racket is smuggling arms and drugs. Maybe antiquities, too."

The press conference began with Dr. Grassley summarizing the stele's discovery and excavation of the dwelling. The archeologists provided translations of the stele's three inscriptions. As Grassley thanked Vivian for providing the translation of the Celtic inscription, she wondered if the downturn at the corners of Dr. Price's mouth was only her imagination.

Grassley acknowledged the possible connection between

the word "Mirdin" on the stele and the Celtic name "Myrddin." From the latter, he pointed out, the name "Merlin" was derived. Though not endorsing any hypothesis, the team noted the frescos could certainly argue for a Western European connection. Without mentioning the possibility that Mirdin was, in some sense, the individual known as Merlin, Grassley and his team left the question hanging heavily in the air.

Grassley's deliberate skirting of the warning she'd given him irritated Vivian. So far, though, she acknowledged it was a deft performance. While the excitement the team generated would be great for publicity and funding, they stopped just shy of saying anything that could get them academically drawn and quartered.

"In the days following excavation of the dwelling," Grassley continued, "We uncovered a tablet dealing with Mirdin and his departure homeward from Sogdia."

That was news to Vivian. Sitting straight in her chair, she gave her fullest attention to the proceedings.

"This tablet adds," Grassley explained, "that when Mirdin left, he took with him what the tablet refers to as 'his great treasure.' It also includes a detailed description, a kind of riddle, of the area where Mirdin intended to build his tomb. In theory, the tomb's location could be pinpointed by matching the tablet's description with known landmarks. So far, we have been unable to make such a connection."

Together, Grassley, Abdulin, and Price yanked the black cloth off the display table. It revealed an unassuming tablet of baked clay, not much larger than a paperback book. The sound of a hundred cameras and phones taking photos at once filled the room.

What Grassley and his team called the Treasure Tablet was also engraved with tripartite inscriptions in Sogdian, Manichean, and Celtic written in Roman script. Clearly, this was the surprise Grassley teased her with during her first night in Samarkand. She couldn't imagine why he hadn't invited her to examine the Celtic this time. Was he more jealous and territorial than she realized?

44

After the team presented the Treasure Tablet, they opened the conference for questions. The room erupted in bedlam.

Vivian cringed as the journalists seized upon the Merlin angle. Many were incredulous but a few seemed, instead, far too credulous. The treasure hunters, in contrast, displayed pure pragmatism. Where is the treasure? How do you get there? Do you know what kind of treasure? Grassley politely rebuffed such questions, repeating that they just didn't know yet. If the hunters persisted, Dr. Abdulin's baleful stare silenced them.

The academics were the worst. Like circling sharks, each was determined to be the one responsible for discrediting the archeologists' claims. Even with limited information, the other scholars confidently proclaimed that the frescoes must be of the Aral Sea, or the team had dated the site incorrectly, or translated the inscriptions erroneously.

Even Vivian was not immune. Not having examined the Treasure Tablet, she asked some pointed questions about why the team assumed the tablet was Insular Celtic rather that the extinct Continental Celtic. She also emphasized the risks of reading too much into transliterations of proper nouns. Vivian kept to herself the fact that she had spent much of the past week doing precisely that.

As a linguist droned on about a minor point of Sogdian grammar, Vivian's attention drifted. It came roaring back with the cacophony of doors crashing open and the sounds of gunfire and screaming filling the conference room.

A dozen men stormed into the room, their olive drab uniforms lacking names or insignias. Bandanas concealed their faces. Guns leveled and firing, they secured the main door and then rushed towards the display table and the tablet.

Throwing herself to the ground when the first gunshots sounded, Vivian kept her head down but eyes and ears open. The screams, she noted, were screams of fear, not pain. Risking lifting her head just a little, she saw few actual injuries as she scanned the room. The gunfire seemed intended to frighten rather than kill. Vivian began paying careful attention to the events unfolding around her.

She watched in fascination as a treasure hunter, "Booker" she thought Grassley called him, calmly stuck his leg out in front of the lead gunman. As the gunman tripped over the treasure hunter's dusty cowboy boot, he stumbled and slowed. The remaining gunmen piled up behind him, struggling to keep their footing.

Their focus was on the display table. It was clear what the gunmen were after. Vivian kicked off her heels, the better to run with, and dashed madly toward the table. Before the gunmen fully recovered from their collision, she grabbed the Treasure Tablet. Sprinting through a side door, Vivian's peripheral vision saw the assailants following her.

In the lobby, Vivian crouched behind a potted plant, trying to remain unseen as she pondered her next move. From behind, a hand pressed lightly upon her shoulder. It was the cowboy treasure hunter, an index finger held firmly to his lips. Face-to-face, she took a good look at Jake Booker. A mane of silver hair framed a craggy face and pale blue eyes. A trim, athletic frame testified that treasure hunting kept him in good shape.

He motioned for Vivian to follow. On impulse, she resolved to trust him, for now. They were almost outside the hotel before the gunmen spotted them and gave chase.

Rushing across the street and weaving through the heavy, creeping traffic of one of Samarkand's busiest roads, the cowboy led them onto a vacant construction site. The steel skeleton of a large building stood unfinished and abandoned in the sweltering summer heat. Building materials and tools remained scattered haphazardly about. As they ran under the building's metal frame, the cowboy rounded on their pursuers. Laying one gunman out with a solid uppercut, he grappled messily with the other. He wasn't losing the brawl but didn't seem able to gain the upper hand, either.

As their fight continued, a third figure clad in olive drab fatigues arrived. Drawing his submachine gun, he ignored Vivian and pointed it toward the melee. Amid the chaos and close-quarters grappling, he was unable to get a clear shot at the cowboy. Irritated by the gunman's complete disregard for her presence, Vivian noted a length of metal pipe on the ground.

The treasure hunter finally incapacitated his other opponent. Looking back, his eyes traveled to the third gunman, unconscious on the ground, and then to the pipe in Vivian's hands. He looked at her quizzically.

"What, you're the only one who can rough up a goon?"

"I didn't say anything." He dusted off his hat. "Jake Booker." He extended his hand.

"Dr. Vivian Cuinnsey," she said, making certain to give a firm, confident handshake.

Hoping to avoid further encounters, they exited through the opposite side of the construction site. A black sedan roared to a stop in front of them. As its doors flew open, more gunmen got out.

"Why don't you step into my office?" Vivian cringed at the slight melodic trill of the voice from inside the sedan.

Chapter Nine

Dr. Price's smile appeared courteous. The smile of the gunmen next to him, less so.

"The Treasure Tablet, please?" asked the archeologist.

With no real alternative, Vivian took the heavy clay piece from her purse and handed it over. As the car made its way through Samarkand's streets, the guards kept their weapons trained on her and Jake. She tried not to think about whether the guns' safeties were on. If the answer was no, given the state of Samarkand's roads, the results could be messy.

"I don't get it," she told their captor, "You're a principle investigator on the team that discovered the tablet. You'd have access to it any time you want. Why go through all of this?"

"I have my reasons."

She thought back to the strange exchange they'd had last night outside of Mirdin's dwelling. "It's the treasure, isn't it? You think it's real."

Price kept his silence.

Something else clicked into place for Vivian. "You're the one behind the thefts, aren't you? You're the mole."

"As it turns out, mercenaries aren't cheap. I needed a way to fund today's activities. Regrettably, your actions have complicated matters." Price held up a hand and the sedan came to a halt.

Departing the vehicle, he added, "I can't allow the two of you to connect me with this. My associates are going to take you for a long ride into the desert."

They rode in silence until reaching the edge of Samarkand. In what she assumed to be Uzbek, Jake spoke to the gunmen. They broke into broad grins. A few moments later, the sedan made a U-turn and headed back into the city.

"You speak Uzbek?" Vivian asked.

"I try to pick up the language anywhere I do business. It shows respect for local partners. And it's a good way to watch my ass by being aware of what, and who, is being talked about."

"What did you say to them?"

"Seven little words that I've found extremely useful, 'Whatever he's paying you, I'll double it.'"

"Oh? And what if the person cutting the paycheck is female?"

For a moment, Jake Booker looked a bit sheepish.

They returned to the hotel. The press conference, obviously, was over. The chaos of its premature ending remained very much in evidence. Price, of course, had already vanished. Vivian checked on the other archeologists. Dr. Grassley sustained some nasty bruises from taking a hard fall during the attack. Hopefully, nothing permanent.

Dr. Abdulin was in shock. She had just received word from the dig site that every record of the Treasure Tablet there had been deleted or destroyed. Several local excavators were unaccounted for. Local excavators, it bore mentioning, who had been particularly close to Price. When Vivian informed her that Price was behind the tablet's theft, and presumably also the vandalism at the excavation, Dr. Abdulin's mood soured to a stony-faced rage.

When Vivian located the cowboy again, he was speaking with another of the treasure hunters, the small man wearing the very big uniform. Jake motioned her over. "Dr. Cuinnsey, allow me to present General Gumanizov."

The general took her hand with a grip surprisingly light and delicate. Bowing to kiss it, as the long rows of medals on his uniformed dangled downward, Vivian feared they might pull the man over.

"I assure you," he pledged, "I will do everything in my power to ensure that Dr. Price does not leave Uzbekistan. I want him apprehended and the Treasure Tablet recovered as badly as you do." Gumanizov's charm was oily as a two-day old fish. That did not make it ineffective.

"Thank you," Vivian replied.

"Our international airports are apprised of the situation," he continued, "as Price must expect. I believe he'll attempt to

49

leave overland. I can best monitor that from my headquarters in Surxondaryo, where I'm close to the borders with Afghanistan, Tajikistan, and Turkmenistan." The general paused. "The two of you are welcome to come with me and enjoy my hospitality as you witness operations from there."

"How long until you leave?" Jake asked.

"I depart within the hour."

"I expect Dr. Cuinnsey would need to check in with her university to apprise them on the situation before she makes a decision." While Jake spoke his words to the general, his eyes contained a separate message for Vivian. "Yes, you do."

Vivian nodded in agreement and the pair moved away from the second treasure hunter. Turning to Jake, Vivian spoke, "Nice move. I assume you want to talk privately?"

The cowboy nodded. "Hopefully I wasn't quite that transparent to Gumanizov. Before I started talking with good general," Vivian did not miss the sarcasm in his voice, "I spoke with the regular authorities. They know about Price and will do everything they can. But, honestly, I wouldn't expect much. Anyone who planned all of this will have his exit from the country well planned, too. Gumanizov isn't the only bet but he's the best bet."

"Jake, I don't want to be rude, but what's your angle in all of this?" Vivian demanded.

"Fair question," he replied. "I listened to your questions during the press conference. And you had the cojones to grab the tablet and run for it. If I were a betting man, and I am, I'd say you're the one who can find whatever that tablet leads to. Given recent events, I figure you might be in the market for a partner."

"That's not a bad idea. But I'm an academic. Even if I do find anything, there are professional standards I have to follow. I can't just let you sell off pieces to the highest bidder. I don't see what's in this for you."

Jake smiled, "Let me worry about that. If I can't find a way to make money off this which doesn't involve selling your precious artifacts, I don't deserve to."

She thought that over, "Okay. Tentatively, yes."

They shook on it.

"Back to Gumanizov," Vivian continued. "Price wants the tablet to look for Mirdin's treasure, whatever the hell that is. For the moment, let's assume such a thing exists. I'll stake every degree I've earned that it's not in Uzbekistan. So, Price is either leaving now or he will leave soon." She paused, refining her thoughts. "Based on what we've seen of Price, he's methodical. I agree with you about him having a solid plan for getting out of the country. He may be doing so right now. My question for you is how good is Gumanizov? How much do we need him?"

"If Price is still in the country, and slips up, Gumanizov has the network to notice and, maybe, catch him." It was Jake's turn to gather his thoughts. "More than that, the general is someone I'd prefer to have where I can keep an eye on him. There's no doubt he'll do whatever he can to recover that tablet before it leaves Uzbekistan. Whether Gumanizov would tell us if he gets his hands on it is another question entirely. It will be harder to keep us in the dark if we're by his side."

This was definitely not business as usual for a university departmental chair. After the day's events, Vivian wanted to know how much risk Jake's proposal would put them in.

"I don't believe the man would leave us dead in the desert the way Price planned to. I wouldn't bet my life on it." Jake chuckled morbidly, "Actually, I guess I am. But, even if he wouldn't kill us, the man is shady. You need to understand that. Still," the treasure hunter paused, "you know the old proverb about keeping your friends close and your enemies closer?"

Vivian wondered if that proverb applied to Jake Booker as well as to General Gumanizov. "You think we should go with him?"

"I do. But keep your eyes open. Let's exchange contact information so we can text if there's anything we need to communicate without risk of being overheard. If you see, hear, even smell, something that doesn't seem right, no matter how trivial, I want to know about it. Okay?"

Jake stopped. Perhaps realizing he sounded patronizing, his tone softened. "You're tough and you're smart, I've seen that. But don't forget this guy has been playing for keeps a lot longer than you have."

Vivian nodded, thinking Jake had never seen an interdepartmental budget meeting.

An hour later, Vivian and Jake stood with Gumanizov and his entourage on hotel's roof. A massive helicopter gunship perched menacingly on the helipad like a giant metal bird of prey. A nasty looking cannon protruded below the craft's nose. *Its beak*, Vivian thought. Pods brimming with rockets and missiles danged from two stubby wings. But its color, glossy black instead of mottled camouflage or green, made Vivian think of a flying, death-dealing limousine.

As it turned out, that is precisely what it was.

"This is my pride and joy," Gumanizov proclaimed with the look of a five-year old describing a favorite toy. "A Mi-24 'Hind' gunship, customized to my personal specifications by the Mil Corporation of Russia. Their CEO is a good friend of mine."

As the general explained the helicopter's various modifications and customizations, Vivian watched Jake talk with its pilot. A vigorous, ruddy-complexioned man with thinning white hair and a bushy mustache, his custom flight suit looked more appropriate to a World War I flyboy than a twenty-first century helicopter pilot. What she really noticed was the "thousand yard stare" in his blue eyes, the gaze of someone who had witnessed his share of death and destruction, and not as a bystander.

Jake looked at one of the helicopter's two single-person cockpits as the pilot, gesturing and pointing, explained something to him.

"Normally, the Hind carries eight soldiers," Gumanizov said, hoping to reclaim Vivian's attention. "I had the company replace the troop compartment with this," as Gumanizov nodded, one of his guards opened a door in the fuselage. It revealed a luxury suite with red velvet curtains on its windows, leather couches, a mini-bar, gaming console, and state of the art sound system. The general beamed with pride.

As they flew over Samarkand's outlying neighborhoods, Vivian's phone buzzed with an incoming text. Jake was already putting her contact information to use.

"When the general says this helicopter is his pride and joy, he means that literally. It's his personal toy, not part of the Uzbek military."

"Interesting," she texted. *"Most people are content with a company car. Who's the pilot?"*

"Rodchenko. He was a hotshot pilot for the Russians back when they were the ones in Afghanistan. Gumanizov hired him away as his personal chauffer. From what I hear, Rodchenko also uses the copter when the general needs to slap down rival smugglers or the occasional police patrol."

"Friend of yours?"

"Hardly. But I've been taking copter lessons. It's not often I get to look at a machine like this one."

Vivian put away her phone, not wanting to give Gumanizov cause for suspicion because she and Jake were texting simultaneously. Picking up on her ruse, the treasure hunter continued texting for several minutes, as if he had been talking with someone else the entire time.

Flying south, the landscape grew more fertile. Broken desert gave way to open grassland and thin woodland. "What kind of trees are those?" Vivian wanted to know.

"Mostly pistachio," Gumanizov replied, "Some almond, apple, and juniper. Walnut, too."

An hour after leaving Samarkand, the helicopter descended toward a small military base around an imposing stone peak. A weathered stone fortress occupied its summit, surrounded by green patches Vivian took for gardens. A large helipad spread over the flatland below. Two helicopters rested there while maintenance crews tended to them, with obvious space for more craft. Anti-aircraft guns and missiles flanked the helipad. Barracks and warehouses, in turn, ringed the weapons. The compound's massive perimeter fence, accentuated by tall guard towers, separated the compound from the surrounding countryside.

"So," Vivian thought, "this is Gumanizov's idea of home."

Chapter Ten

After they landed, a driver ushered the general, Vivian, and Jake into a waiting air-conditioned limousine. Vivian glanced back as they drove away. She saw Rodchenko, hands on his hips, examining the ground crew's work as they tended to the Hind. It appeared he did not approve of what he saw. The pilot, it seemed, took great interest in every aspect of his helicopter.

The limousine drove through the compound, its streets busy with armored vehicles, jeeps, and trucks. Their limo took the winding, switchbacked road leading up the peak toward the stone fortress. What, from the air, Vivian took to be gardens proved to be exactly that. Lush and well-tended in an English county style, they were dotted with fountains, statues, and trestles. The fortress had been extensively renovated. Full-length tinted windows, massive air conditioning units on the roof, and a satellite dish all argued the building was now at least as much villa as castle.

Its interior proved even more ostentatious than the exterior. Gumanizov's steward, a gaunt man who wore his servility like a badge of honor, showed the general's guests to their rooms. The elaborately apportioned quarters given to Vivian put her room in Samarkand, allegedly at one of the country's best hotels, to shame.

For all that, it displeased Vivian that her room and Jake's were in separate wings. Despite the steward's protestations about "modesty and propriety," the rooming arrangements left Vivian uneasy. She remained a long way from trusting a treasure hunter like Jake Booker. But, at least for now, he was *her* treasure hunter.

"The general dines in one hour," the steward proclaimed. "Until then, you are invited to relax and make yourself ready."

Vivian rested on her bed, contemplating what had been strangest day of her life. And it wasn't over yet.

Her phone buzzed. *"Nice rooms, huh?"*

"Yes" she replied to Jake, *"Not so happy being split up, though. Think we'll get a chaperone?"*

"Ha! I don't like it, either. I have a hard time believing our host is deeply concerned with modesty and propriety. Like I said, keep your eyes and ears open."

"At least we're in the middle of an army base."

"Only on paper. I imagine most of the equipment is on the Uzbek army's books. But the men are personally loyal to Gumanizov."

"Oh, thank you. That makes me feel so much better."

Vivian brought one nice outfit with her to Uzbekistan, for the press conference. She had been wearing it for over twelve hours. During that time she'd sprinted, knocked a man unconscious, and been kidnapped. To call the ensemble no longer ideal for a formal dinner was putting it mildly.

Clothes of all shapes and sizes, however filled her room's walk-in closet. She wondered how the general had come by them. Their common thread, Vivian smirked at her own pun, was that each garment was once the height of fashion. Depending on the piece, that might be six months ago, or fifty years. But all of it had, at one time, been haute couture.

Vivian selected a simple, slate-colored cocktail dress. The well-tailored garment was old enough to have come back into fashion. Besides, it matched her eyes. Taking her time, Vivian washed and dressed.

A wave of impressions flooded Vivian's senses as she entered the dining room. Aromas of cooking food wafted in from the adjacent kitchen. In one corner, a string quartet worked their way through a piece by Rimsky-Korsakov. She especially could not ignore the décor. Even by Gumanizov's standards, his dining room represented an exercise in overstatement.

First, there were the antiquities. A complete set of Central Asian armor. Bejeweled swords and daggers. A thousand years of porcelains with elaborate and colorful geometric designs. A numismatic case filled with gold coins stretching from Alexander the Great to the Shahs of Persia. Gumanizov's collection would be the envy of a small college museum. Doubting the Uzbek army paid its generals so well, Vivian remembered Dr. Grassley's musings about Gumanizov's various shadow enterprises.

The room's centerpiece, on the other hand, would never be the envy of collectors. Overshadowing the antiquities and other furnishings, a full length floor-to-ceiling neoclassical oil painting of their host dominated the dining room. With great effort, Vivian suppressed a giggle.

Underneath his portrait, in one-quarter scale, stood the actual Gumanizov. Waving her over, the general introduced Vivian to members of his entourage and hangers-on as well as to a number of "friends" and "business associates" from Afghanistan, China, Russia, Tajikistan, and Turkmenistan.

From the corner of her eye, Vivian observed Jake Booker enter. Donning an old-fashioned, and flatteringly tight, tuxedo, the treasure hunter cleaned up nicely. Noting he hadn't forsaken his cowboy hat or scuffed up boots, she wondered if that reflected vanity or practicality. As he had with Vivian, Gumanizov introduced Jake to his diverse and questionable associates.

Soon after, the general's steward entered the dining room. He struck a small gong, its melodious tone indicated dinner would soon be served and guests should take their seats. Vivian glanced around the long, rectangular table. Instinct pulled her toward an empty seat next to Jake. Yes, for the time being, the cowboy definitely was *her* shady treasure hunter. Nor did it seem all one way. Unless she misread him completely, the treasure hunter appeared relieved, and perhaps pleased, that she took the seat to his left.

A small army of waiters placed steaming plates of food in front of the guests. When everyone had been served, Gumanizov stood. Raising his glass, he offered a toast to his two new guests.

"Thank you. Your place is…fascinating," Vivian said, one of the few comments she could unhesitatingly offer her host, "and such a distinctive building."

"You are very kind," the diminutive general blushed, oblivious to the subtext of Vivian's carefully worded remark.

57

"In the days of the Tsars this fortress housed a Russian Army garrison," he paused, "You see, I am descended from the Khans of Bukhara..."

As the general continued, Vivian gave Jake a sidewise glance to ask "Is that true?" After, with a shrug and display of open palms, the treasure hunter conveyed, "Hell if I know," Vivian returned her attention to Gumanizov's story.

"...When the Russian Empire annexed Bukhara and Samarkand in the nineteenth century, they demolished the beautiful old castle the khans had built on this spot to control the trade routes. Then the Russians raised this one in its place. When I became military commander of the Surxondaryo Region, I took over the abandoned fortress and made it my residence. Call it my little act of revenge."

Though it seemed impolitic to ask, Vivian wondered whom the Khans of Bukhara had replaced. As Dr. Price had observed, civilization had long roots in Central Asia. Only in the great river valleys: the Huang He, Indus, Mesopotamia, and Nile, did it possess a longer pedigree. Stretch this peak's history back far enough and who knew what you'd find. A Sogdian settlement? Dr. Grassley might know. Perhaps Mirdin, whoever he really was, had been here. Before that? A camp for Alexander the Great and his men? A Neolithic hillfort?

"But we are not here to talk about the history of my land," the general apologized. "It is a different place we are interested in. So, Dr. Cuinnsey," as Gumanizov spoke, every face at the table turned toward her, "what are your thoughts on Merlin's treasure? Are we going to find it under Stonehenge or something?"

Vivian laughed politely. Even if she knew anything useful at this point, she would have been reluctant to share it. Luckily, the general's phrasing offered a convenient deflection. "A common misconception," Vivian began an explanation she'd given countless times. "The great stone circles were built about 5,000 years ago. By the time the first Celts came to the British Isles, Stonehenge and her sisters had stood for at least 2,000 years, maybe closer to 3,000."

"Weren't Celts the first inhabitants of Britain, then?"

Again, Vivian found the ground familiar. Not so much "debunking" as gently correcting widely circulated misinformation. "Most experts think Celts originated near the Alps and then spread out. At one point, they stretched from Turkey to Ireland. Most of them were absorbed by other groups moving in from the east and, later, Romans from the south. Eventually, largely because of the terrain and because it was the edge of the known world, the British Isles and Breton Peninsula remained the only places where Celtic languages and cultures continued on."

"And have you always studied dead Celtic languages, like the ones you found here?" Gumanizov inquired.

"Actually, I started with living ones. English is my native language. But, growing up, I learned Manx, which is my ancestral tongue. Then Irish and Scottish Gaelic, which are closely related to Manx. After that, Welsh, Breton, and Cornish, the living Brittonic languages. It wasn't until my doctorate that I looked at the history of those languages and, by extension, the languages they came from.

"For my dissertation, I wanted to study the origins of Manx. Celts from Britain settled the Isle of Man during the Iron Age. They spoke a language related to Welsh. But, in the sixth century, Celts from Ireland started arriving and became the dominant group. When that happened, the island's language changed, too. Eventually, it resembled Irish and Scottish Gaelic more than Welsh. If you look at the Ogham inscriptions on the island, you can actually see the change happen over a century or two."

With skills honed by over a decade of teaching, Vivian sized-up her audience. Most of those at the table tuned out the moment talk turned to history and language. Gumanizov stayed focused at the beginning of her answers. But, when she went into depth, his attention wandered. Not so with Jake Booker. The cowboy's eyes remained bright and attentive throughout her commentary. It was the gaze of a student heading toward, at least, a B+.

"I wanted to know how much influence that earlier Brittonic Manx language had on modern Manx," Vivian continued. "When I started researching, I found it very difficult to proceed without first answering another question. Beginning with Viking raids in the ninth century, Scandinavians dominated the Isle of Man for 500 years. It is a valid question whether the Manx language really survived the occupation or if what we think of as modern Manx was something introduced after the Scandinavians left.

"With help from my colleagues in the archeology and history departments, that's what my dissertation ended up examining. Linguistic research is rarely decisive. Usually, it crawls rather than sprints. My dissertation showed that some of the old Manx language survived Scandinavian occupation. But establishing how much, and exactly what, survived could take years, maybe generations."

"I find remarkable that dead languages can be translated," the general observed, "When you saw the…" he fumbled for the proper term, "…stele, how did you make sense of it? Explain it to me."

"Some of my colleagues wouldn't like me saying this, but translations like the stele are part science…and part art," she began.

"If two modern languages share a common trait in their structure, word order, or grammar, it's a good bet any parent languages they share also possessed that trait. The same thing applies to vocabulary, if words in related languages sound similar, they probably sounded similar in parent languages too.

"Take the word 'mother.' In Spanish, it's *madre*. It's the same in Italian. And, in French, it's *mère,* not very different. All three of those languages evolved from Latin, where the word for mother is *mater*. Do you see?" smiling politely, Vivian wondered if Gumanizov really did.

"But you have to be careful," she cautioned, "Just because two words sound the same doesn't necessarily mean they are related. Take *nine*. In German, it means 'no.' It English, it's the number between eight and ten. They're pronounced identically. They're spelled almost the same, 'n-i-n-e' in English and 'n-e-i-n' in German. But, even though English and German share a parent language, the meanings are different.

"But, if I have a good idea of what extinct language I'm looking at, I can use common traits of languages that descend from it to translate at least some of the extinct one. I was confident the stele was written in Common Brittonic. Because I know Welsh, Breton, and some Cornish, which all evolved from Common Brittonic, I could work backward from those and understand a lot of the stele.

"That's the 'science' part," Vivian observed, "With a language that's been extinct a long time, especially when there are gaps in our understanding of what came between it and its modern descendants, a linguist needs a combination of great research skills, inspired guesswork, and good instincts. That's the 'art' part."

"And you could do the same thing with the Treasure Tablet?" Gumanizov asked enthusiastically.

She replied with circumspection. Translation, Vivian thought, was not the only time instincts proved useful. "That depends. The language on the tablet hasn't been used in almost 1,500 years. Some words won't be decipherable because they've changed too much between parent and child languages. There may also be shifts in grammar we don't understand. Things like allusions and slang may be utterly lost on us because we lack the cultural knowledge required to deduce their meaning."

Every word of her reply was completely true. Technically. Vivian, however, never lacked for confidence. She knew her translations seldom missed the mark by much, no matter how much art went into them. The general, however, did not need to know that.

Chapter Eleven

In the early years of Myrddin's service to Tarkun, the king
suggested his new grand vizier experience more of Sogdia
directly. The idea made sense. Like Arthur before him,
Tarkun was an astute ruler with his own measure of wisdom.
It was part of what drew the wizard to both of them. After
Myrddin agreed to Tarkun's proposal the monarch would
periodically dispatch him on small missions throughout the
kingdom.

The small community of Iskachek, on Sogdia's fringes,
had not delivered its seasonal tax assessment. Or, at least, the
assessment had not arrived in the capital. Iskachek had never
been troublesome and, suspecting no malice on the town's
part, Tarkun sent Myrddin to investigate.

The scale of Sogdia, indeed of many kingdoms east of
Constantinople, still awed Myrddin. In the distance between
Tarkun's court and Iskachek, he could travel from Cornwall
to the land of the Picts. How many small kingdoms of the
Britons and Saxons would fit into those leagues?

Within a fertile valley, Iskachek nestled around a rocky
spur crowned by a small citadel. Myrddin's caution, earned
over more than half a lifetime spent in fractious, unpredictable
Britain, served him well. Coming upon the town
circumspectly, Myrddin found its fields despoiled, buildings
burned, and the citadel barred for siege. Hundreds of the long-
haired, flat-faced horsemen surrounded the rock spur. They
came from north of Sogdia. Myrddin often warned Tarkun
about them. Still mostly a nuisance, he sensed in them the
potential to become everything the Saxons had been. And
much more.

It would have been easy enough to return to the capital and
dispatch a relief force. Myrddin wanted more. He needed to
know the conditions of those besieged within the citadel.
Concealing himself and his steed some distance away, he
waited until nightfall. Myrddin donned a black cloak and
darkened his face, neck, and hands with charcoal. All but

invisible by night, Myrddin slipped through the horsemen's lines and into the citadel.

Iskachek's besieged residents welcomed him. Fate had been kind. The dust clouds raised by the raiders gave ample warning. By far the greater part of the population reached the citadel safely. But, in that kindness was cruelty. Though a natural spring lay tantalizingly just beyond the horseman's camp. But the weather gods had been parsimonious. The citadel's cistern was low. Examining the water supply and counting the crowd within the fortress, Myrddin estimated the townspeople had a week's water, maybe less. Even if he left now, a relief force might not arrive in time.

Realizing he must work with what was at hand, Myrddin took stock of his assets. Much of the town's guard perished buying their friends and family time to reach the citadel. Only a handful remained. Even then, Myrddin acknowledged, they were not real warriors, only farmers, artisans, and traders who held a weapon a couple of times a year.

Fortunately, one true warrior waited within the walls, serendipitously at Iskachek when the horsemen came. Mari was one of Myrddin's favorites, second only to Tarkun in his affection. A champion in the king's guard, she equaled of any of Arthur's knights. Her steed, Rakhsha, outran any horse in the kingdom. Magic reputedly dwelled in Mari's scimitar. But it was her shield the poets sang of, hardened camel hide stretched across a stout wooden frame. Emblazed with iron studs in the shape of her god's cross, she claimed it provided a more than earthly protection.

True, the Celts and Saxons had their shield maidens. The Goths had their Valkyries, like dear Areagne, the Brown Hild, whom he had taught early in his wanderings. But such fighters were unusual. Among the Sogdians, as with the Bactrians, Circassians, Sarmatians, and Scythians, the ranks of their archers and cavalry swelled with women. Myrddin approved.

Gwynhumara, of course, would have been surprised to hear that. She had often called him a misogynist. Nothing could be further from the truth. But he had known no polite way to tell his queen, and the wife of his dearest friend, that he respected all women...of character and intelligence.

The citadel held other assets, for those with the eyes to see them and mind to devise their use. A Sogdian village had more craftspeople than a British town. If he needed them, here were carpenters, masons, smiths, tailors, tanners, and others besides. Foremost among them was Meruz, a master blacksmith, very nearly a hero in his own right. Even Tarkun's court knew of his skill.

Wei was an unexpected addition to the assemblage in the citadel. By this point along the Silk Road, the Sui silk merchants typically passed their cloth on to middlemen. Occasionally, a bold trader like Wei traveled further, hoping to keep more profit for himself. Caught in the siege, he and his precious fabric now sheltered in the citadel. Myrddin wondered if Wei regretted his decision.

Myrddin didn't.

Crafting his plan to save Iskachek, he reflected that ideas were circles within in circles. Wei's presence gave him the idea. But it would not have occurred to him had it not been for his epic flight from Nimue's, attempting to reach Camlann in time. That idea, in turn, arose from long ago conversations with Bleys.

It would be a conjuration, of sorts. The grandest one he had ever attempted. And it would require every bit of talent sheltered within the citadel's walls to pull it off.

Immediately, Myrddin set Meruz and the other smiths to work, along with the town's carpenters and tanners. He then conferred with Mari.

The smiths toiled day and night. Aside from a few swords and axes set carefully aside, the artisans sharpened anything with an edge, point, or hook and mounted it to a long pole with a band of iron and two stout rivets. Tanners strung raw leather and hide over wooden frames, boiling them until they reached nearly the strength of metal. The carpenters too, worked diligently to meet Myrddin's unusual request.

He helped Mari train the Sogdians. For all his wizardry and her martial skill, the plan required more fighters of flesh and blood. Of necessity, they made do with anyone who could follow orders and hold a weapon and shield. Men and women. Nobles and beggars. Beardless adolescents and grayhairs little younger than Myrddin. Even if they had horses and bows to spare, time didn't allow training the townspeople into riders and archers. They would have to fight the horsemen on foot. Fortunately, Myrddin knew of a people who excelled in precisely that kind of fighting. He dusted off what he learned from the old Romans so many decades ago.

As Mari schooled the townspeople in the arts of one-on-one combat, he asked her to select a dozen of the best. Taking those twelve aside, Myrddin distributed the town's few swords and axes to them. They would be his tiny reserve force in the impending battle.

Myrddin drilled the remainder in tactics. He distributed the tanners' shields to the men and women. "Look at your shield," he began, "It is not for you. It is for the person to your left. The shield to your right is not for the one holding it, it is yours. You depend upon each other. You fight as one. You will succeed or fail as one."

He then passed out the long pole weapons made by the blacksmiths, keeping one for himself. "You may ask yourself, 'How will a craftsman, a merchant, a farmer on foot triumph over a mounted warrior?'" Merlin drove the butt of his weapon against the ground. "You will brace your weapon against the earth. It is not your strength that will power it. It is the Earth's strength. What you should be asking yourself is 'How can the horsemen hope to triumph over the Earth itself?'"

He had at least one thing going for him. With fewer notions about warfare's nobility and, consequently, less emphasis on individual glory, the Sogdians were easier to train in tactics than the Britons had been.

Myrddin drilled the townspeople by day. In the evening, he supervised the artisans. Fortunately, Myrddin needed less sleep than others. Half the normal span sufficed. Over brief intervals, he could make do with a quarter span and suffer no ill effects to health or cognition.

At night, working by moonlight, he isolated himself atop the citadel's tallest tower. Alone, he blended brimstone and charcoal, materials easy to find, with the rare white crystals he'd gathered from caves at every opportunity since leaving China. Funneling the resulting dark, grainy admixture into a tube of lacquered paper, he secreted it where it would be safe from both damp and flame.

Not long after, the carpenters completed their task. Myrddin examined the curved, graceful wooden frame. He complimented the artisans on the work. No doubt they had grown sick of his contradictory instructions that it must be both light and strong. And rightly so. That did not render his request any less essential. He then set the tailors to work. Wei cringed as they cut apart his precious stock, sewing it into shapes ruining its commercial value. But, presumably, the merchant loved his silk less than his life.

When the tailors finished, only one thing remained. With heavy heart, Myrddin went to Mari to discuss her role.

The plan required the perfect weather. They waited. And waited. With each passing day, the cistern grew lower and the people more fearful. Then came a dawn when the cistern held only dampness. One way or another, they had to act today. Just when Myrddin feared they could delay no longer, the weather shifted. Hot, dry winds blew from the south. Strong-backed townspeople carried Myrddin's creation, its green silk stretched over a curved wooden frame, to the battlements.

The great green dragon flew from the citadel's walls. It was less glorious than Myrddin's escape from Nimue, but magnificent nonetheless. Updrafts of warm air held the creature aloft, almost stationary. Its wings appeared to flap in the breeze as it hovered over the horsemen. Far below, their lines grew tenuous as warriors that feared no human foe shifted nervously in saddles. Fearfully, their horses regarded the strange predator above them, its wingspan as wide as five men. Discipline and iron leadership held the lines for now. The horsemen's captain ordered bows drawn and a volley of arrows fired at the monster.

Myrddin watched them pass through his "dragon" with only a modicum of worry. So long as they didn't damage the wooden frame too badly or strike the lacquered paper tube, passing through the silk would do no harm.

Within the dragon, a horsehair fuse burned slowly down to the lacquered paper tube. Myrddin prayed to whatever gods listened that the fuse neither went out nor caught the dragon's silk skin on fire. The beast's head lowered, its bottom jaw distending. A thick column of fire medicine poured from its gaping maw, blazing, sparkling, and booming as it descended toward the ground.

For many horseman, that proved too much. Dust rose from the Sogdian plain as they fled. When the dust settled, Merlin counted. Perhaps two in three of the horseman had gone. He hoped for more, but, running numbers in his head, calculated that victory remained possible. More than that, he knew it in his heart.

As Myrrdin shouted, townspeople threw open the citadel's gates. With a bloodcurdling war cry worthy of the Morrigan, Mari galloped forth on Rakhsha. Speeding down the hill, her tightly gripping legs anchored her to her steed. As she rode, Mari launched a flurry of arrows at the horsemen's captain. The third shot found its mark. The captain slid from his mount, arrow shaft protruding from his face.

The fallen captain's honor guard charged Mari. She continued loosing arrows, felling several. Mari sheathed her bow as the first two guards reached her. Drawing scimitar and shield, she quickly slew them. Other horseman joined the decimated honor guard in charging the Sogdian champion. As another pair reached her, she dispatched them as well. Four others arrived, raining their blades down upon her. It took all her effort to block them, the studded cross on her shield gleaming brilliantly in the sunlight. She slew two with blows of opportunity. Their places were quickly taken, and more besides.

Surrounded by eight horsemen, the end came quickly. Mercifully, Myrddin could not see the killing blow. He only saw Mari's body fall, lifeless, to the earth, her blood seeping into the thirsty ground. It had been a suicide mission. Myrddin knew that. Mari had known it as well. But it had been necessary. Not only to take out the horsemen's captain, and a dozen others as it turned out, but to break the horsemen's formation as they met her charge.

Amid the distraction of her final charge, Myrrdin had moved his troops out of the gate and formed them into a square on the slope leading to the citadel.

Taking command of his fellows, one of the horsemen ordered a charge. Closing with the Sogdians, they loosed a volley of arrows.

"Shields up," Myrddin commanded. He took no cover as he stood amidst the people of Iskachek. It put him at risk, but he had to display unflinching courage to the others. If he survived, he suspected the townspeople's morale would hold. If he fell, they would break, and fall, with him. Myrddin heard the distinctive whoosh of an arrow landing near him. Then another. And another. Then a fourth. None found his flesh.

A half-dozen Sogdians fell from the rain of arrows, most never to rise again. "Brace your weapons," Myrddin shouted as the horsemen closed at a full gallop. "Remember, the Earth is your strength. The Earth is your strength!"

Myrddin had known his share of battlefields. Few sounds were more terrible than the crash of metal and flesh together, mingled with the screams of men and horses. When the first dreadful instant passed, only a few horsemen, looking much the worse for wear, had penetrated their square. Myrddin dispatched his reserves. Fighters with swords and axes descended upon those riders. Pulling them from their horses, they made short work of their foes. More Sogdians had fallen along the lines of the square. But less than Myrddin expected. In most places, the square held, horsemen and their mounts strewn before them.

The surviving riders regrouped, swinging around in a wide arc. Anticipating another charge, Myrddin exhorted the townspeople to reform their lines. Instead, the remaining horsemen departed northward as a victory cry rose form the Sogdians.

In the aftermath, Myrddin knelt beside Mari, weeping silently as the priests prepared her body for burial. While he had no idea what possible use a sword or bow would have in the Nestorian's tranquil afterlife, Myrddin would never take a fallen warrior's weapons. A shield was another matter. He hoped Mari would not begrudge her friend a token to remember her by.

Chapter Twelve

After dinner, Vivian sat on the edge of her bed, reflecting on the evening. No one would ever call Gumanizov an original thinker. But the man was not stupid. Sooner or later, he would realize that, if he got his hands on the Treasure Tablet, he needed someone around to decipher it. Dinner conversation suggested the general had already groped pretty far in that direction. His questions had felt like a job interview. It was a job Vivian did not want. And Gumanizov did not seem like a person to let something, or someone, he required wander freely out of his front door.

She needed to get out of here while she still could.

Of course, everything which could be said about the general could also be said of Jake Booker. Vivian tried to figure out why he was different or, at least, felt different. The cowboy had been upfront about what he wanted and open to defining their partnership's terms. And he had been useful. Of course, that was in his self-interest.

It would be nice not to be beholden to anyone. At least until she returned to Samarkand. There, she could examine her position with a clear head and negotiate from a position of strength and safety. The question was, could she make an escape on her own?

Vivian turned the issue over in her mind. Unsurprisingly, as a linguist, her decision hinged on a matter of language. Somewhere between here and Samarkand, she would likely have to talk with someone. For directions. Food. Water. Even, heaven forbid, medical attention. English might work, but, from what she had seen, she would not want to chance it. Breton? Irish? Scots Gaelic? Welsh? The idea was absurd. Vivian couldn't trust that she would be able to communicate with locals. But Jake Booker could.

With a sigh, she pulled out her phone, *"Awake?"*

"Yep."

"We need to get out of here," Vivian said, texting the treasure hunter an abridged version of her worries about Gumanizov.

"OK. You've sold me on it. What's your plan?"

Vivian wanted to tell Jake that, as the treasure hunter, formulating a plan should be his job. Instead she texted, *"Sneak out of the compound? Maybe stowaway in a truck or steal a jeep?"*

"Nothing for 100 miles in any direction. Even if we steal a vehicle, he'd catch us in his damn helicopter."

"OK. We disable the helicopter. Or we steal it, Mr. I'm-taking-helicopter-lessons." In the pause that followed, Vivian grew nervous awaiting a response.

"I like how you think, Doc." Another pause, *"Meet me in the garden."*

"Won't that make G. suspicious?"

"Nah. We're in the middle of his military base. It won't occur to him we're considering ducking out and taking his fancy toy with us until it's too late. Hopefully."

"OK."

"Give me twenty minutes."

Vivian scavenged the walk-in closet, finding clothes and, more importantly, shoes more practical for a midnight escape than what she'd worn for the press conference or dinner. She then grabbed the rest of her belongings and exited.

Under different circumstances, the garden and the warm, dry evening air would have been lovely. Instead, Vivian sweated from tension. She hated the way two of Gumanizov's guards kept eyeing her. They hadn't said or done anything indicating she was not supposed to be in the garden. But, clearly, they found it unusual. And they were right. When the cowboy missed the twenty minute mark, it further put her nerves on edge.

"Sorry I'm late, I had a few calls to make," Jake said, appearing from the darkness. She wanted to ask to whom, but they launched into planning the details of their escape instead. When they finished, Vivian indicated the guards. "How do we slip away from those two?"

Jake considered the question. "We don't. Just walk away. Walk with confidence, like nothing funny's going on."

Strolling out of the garden and down the road to the bottom of the hill, Vivian forced herself to appear nonchalant. It must have worked. The guards exchanged looks as she and Jake departed but took no other action.

At the helipad, a single soldier stood guard over the Hind. He stiffened at their approach, raising his weapon slightly. Plotting in the garden, Vivian's first thought had been to tell the guard that she left her purse in the helicopter. That felt cliché. Taking a minute, she crafted a more respectable and persuasive alternative.

She smiled warmly at the guard. "I left my laptop in helicopter," she said. When he regarded her with incomprehension, Jake translated her statement into Uzbek.

The guard said something and shook his head. Clearly a refusal. Fortunately, Vivian had a plan for doubling-down. "The general really wants to see some data I've got on it. I'd hate to tell him one of his men is holding us up." As Jake translated, Vivian batted her eyes innocently.

She watched the guard's resolve crumble. Taking keys from his pocket, he turned from Jake toward the helicopter and opened the passenger suite's door. Vivian clocked him in the head.

She was no street fighter. She should have improvised a club, as she had in Samarkand. The guard quickly shook off the blow. But, surprised and confused, his attention focused on her. That was a mistake. Jake delivered a solid chop to the man's throat. Putting a hand over the guard's mouth to ensure he wouldn't cry out, a second hit rendered him unconscious.

The next part of the plan had been Jake's idea. A way to buy some extra time. Locating the fire extinguisher in the passenger suite, Vivian discharged it. A gray-white cloud drifted from the helicopter. With a little luck, it would be mistaken for smoke. Nobody wanted to get near a burning aircraft, especially one with weapons. Even in a worst-case scenario, it should confuse other guards for a little while.

"Crap!" Jake exclaimed from the tarmac. That couldn't be good.

"What?"

"The guard only has keys for the passenger compartment. Not the cockpits."

Vivian replied with expletives of her own. Her off-color commentary was interrupted by an angry shout, presumably in Uzbek, from out on the helipad. When neither she nor Jake responded, the new arrival switched to something distinctly Slavic sounding. Through the thick clouds made by the fire extinguisher, Rodchenko appeared.

Vivian wondered if the pilot ever let his helicopter out of sight. Finding them messing with his craft, the man's face became a mask of red rage. "What are you doing?"

Jake answered by launching himself at Rodchenko. They rolled around in a bare-knuckles brawl in front of the helicopter. The Russian was older but larger. And very angry. Vivian felt uncertain Jake would come out on top of this one. Taking the empty fire extinguisher canister, she stuck the pilot's head. Groaning, he collapsed on top of the treasure hunter.

"So, that's your signature move?" Jake teased, dragging Rodchenko away from the helicopter.

"What are you doing?" Vivian asked.

"Putting him next to the other guy."

"You're going to leave the crack helicopter pilot here so he can regain consciousness and chase us in one of these other helicopters?"

Jake halted. "Fair point."

Instead, they pulled the unconscious Rodchenko into the Hind's passenger compartment and ripped the velvet curtains from the craft's windows. Using them to gag the pilot and bind his hands and feet, they laid him across a couch.

Rodchenko's appearance proved a blessing in disguise. The pilot had the keys they required for the Hind's twin cockpits. Unlocking them, Jake climbed into the pilot's seat as Vivian settled into the gunner's cockpit ahead of him. Behind her, Vivian heard the treasure hunter running through a preflight checklist "Engage electrical system and hydraulics. Release rotor break. Start left turbine. Open left fuel shutoff valve. Start right turbine. Open right fuel shutoff valve…" His slow and deliberate moves suggested he had done this fewer times than Vivian liked.

The Hind began rocking violently back and forth as its rotors built speed. She didn't remember that from their takeoff in Samarkand. On the other hand, she had also been distracted by Gumanizov's running commentary. "Is it supposed to do that?" Vivian wanted to know.

"I hope so…" Jake replied.

In a few seconds, the rocking ceased. Another worry took its place. Perhaps "smoke" from the fire extinguisher was clearing. Maybe the guards just grew bolder. Either way, a dozen men with assault rifles began stalking across the helipad, closing in on the copter.

"Can you get this damn thing in the air?" Vivian pled.

"If want you her to stay in air," Jake replied, "the RPMs need to build more." She could hear the tension in his voice, too. "We need a little more time."

Vivian had played her fair share of video games. She knew the purpose of the giant stick in front of the gunner's seat. Careful not to depress any of the multitude of buttons on what was effectively an overgrown joystick, Vivian took the control in hand. Moving it vertically and laterally, the mechanical purr of servos and gears rewarded her efforts as the helicopter's main gun swung back and forth and up and down.

With a chorus of alarm, the soldiers surrounding the copter turned tail and fled. Some even dropped their weapons in the rush.

"That buy us enough time?" Vivian asked.

"Damn straight it does," Jake said.

Moments later, he engaged the throttle and they lifted into the night. The Hind roared over Gumanizov's military base, building altitude as they streaked away into the darkness of the Uzbek countryside.

About ten minutes after takeoff, a voice crackled across their radio. Though she couldn't understand the words, it sounded angry and, Vivian thought, familiar.

"Gumanizov?"

"Oh, yeah," Jake grinned, "and is he pissed. Apparently he's forgotten all about needing you and is giving orders to shoot us down."

Chapter Thirteen

"And you're smiling about that?"

"If I were a betting man, and I am, I'd say we don't need to worry." Sensing her skepticism, he elaborated. "Think of it this way. If everyone who could open fire on us doesn't, they all get a slap on the wrist. But if someone shoots us down and temperamental old Gumanizov has a change of heart and throws a tantrum about his favorite toy getting broken, it could go really badly for the man who pulled the trigger. Maybe his family, too, depending on how angry Gumanizov is. So, if you're one his men, what would you do?"

Vivian thought her partner's reasoning was sound. Jake, however, had second thoughts.

"No reason not to hedge our bets, though," he announced, taking the Hind as close to the ground as he dared. That brought dangers of its own. Every so often, he had to pull up fast or bank hard in one direction as buttes, hillocks, ruins, and other hazards emerged suddenly from the darkness. Occasionally, they flew so low over a village that, Vivian thought, if she dangled her arms out of the cockpit, her fingertips would brush the rooftops.

"Are we going back to Samarkand?" Vivian asked.

"Not initially. If the general's not thinking straight, and I'm betting he's too flustered for that, that's what he'll expect us to do. He might put people there to meet us. I've got some natural gas exploration crews in the west of the county. Before we left Gumanizov's, I gave them a call. We're going to link up with them."

"Oh," Vivian said in, she hoped, a neutral tone. His plan was perfectly logical, she admitted. But she felt less than pleased about going from one treasure hunter's clutches to another's. True, Booker had played it straight so far. But she had never been completely in his power. At least until now.

When, a few minutes later Jake said, "*So...*" drawing the word out in the manner of a man about to make confession, she feared the double cross had come. Instead, it was worse than that. "I might have overstated how far along I am in my lessons."

"Meaning what, exactly?"

"Let's just say we want a really broad, flat place to land."

Vivian sighed. "Okay," she resigned herself, "but if we might die in this thing, then there's something I want to do first."

"What?"

Vivian grabbed the gunner's control again, this time depressing its big red trigger with her forefinger. The Hind's Gatling gun fired so rapidly that the noise of individual shots blurred into a continuous roar. Tracer rounds, glowing a brilliant white, streaked into the night like tiny shooting stars. Perhaps it lacked prudence, to say nothing of maturity, but the act was cathartically primal.

She removed her finger from the trigger. "Okay, Mr. Booker. You haven't led us astray so far. Get us down."

A few minutes later, Jake began his descent over a large, dry lakebed. At its center, Vivian spotted another helicopter. Compared with the Hind, it looked like a child's toy. Jake aimed for a spot about fifty yards from the other craft. The only person who could be truly happy with Jake's landing was Vivian's chiropractor. Still, as the old proverb went, any landing you could walk away from was a good one. After Jake powered down the Hind, they exited the copter.

"Should we sabotage the Hind so it can't be used against us?" Vivian asked.

"We've already made a mess of his fancy passenger compartment with the fire extinguisher and embarrassed his golden boy pilot," Jake said. "I'm fine with that. I owe Gumanizov some payback for a very thorny night in Mazar-i-Sharif. But my company still has to do business here. I shouldn't burn my bridges with the general completely."

"Okay. What about Rodchenko, then?"

"What do you think? Should we let him loose?"

Vivian had hoped the treasure hunter wouldn't throw the question back at her. She didn't like the options. Her mind reviled at the idea of leaving him tied up. But, as a practical matter, freeing the pilot brought risks. If he got the heavily armed helicopter airborne again and came after them, then having made it this far would count for nothing.

"I think not. He'll have an unpleasant time," she reasoned, "but it's too dangerous to let him loose. Someone will come along to rescue him eventually. Right?"

Jake nodded. Hoping he was being sincere, she was reassured when he added, "When we're safe, I'll let Gumanizov know where he can find his toy. And his pilot. That will earn us back a few of the brownie points we've lost."

A crew from the second helicopter reached them. "Mr. Booker, Ma'am," one them said. "You folks okay?"

Jake responded with a nod. Vivian replied more colorfully, "Nothing a bottle of wine for me and a few more piloting lessons for Mr. Booker won't fix."

Boarding the other helicopter, she noted a stylized "B.E." on its fuselage, explained below by "Booker Enterprises" in small block letters. The company's copter was a simple utility craft. No, she thought, flying in this, they didn't want Rodchenko coming after them in the Hind. Not at all.

As they took off, Jake turned to her. "Let's get you back to Samarkand."

"Wouldn't it be easier to fly to your operation?"

"It would be," he admitted, "but the general isn't looking for this helicopter. And you've taken a leap of faith trusting me this far. I don't want you to need to worry whether I'll pull a Gumanizov on you."

Vivian wondered if Jake worked that out on his own or if she had been more transparent than she realized.

Dawn was breaking as they touched down at an industrial heliport outside Samarkand. A non-descript company car carried them into the city.

"Do we need to keep worrying about the general?" Vivian asked as they rode.

"I'm not saying stop looking over our shoulders," Jake replied, "but the airport was my biggest worry. It has a strong military presence. That's why we landed at that little heliport. The city itself is pretty far from Gumanizov's powerbase. Trying anything here would be really high profile, especially after what happened with the Treasure Tablet. I think we'll be safe."

Later that morning, they sat down with the other archeologists. Vivian was unsurprised to learn it had been Dr. Price who objected so vociferously to giving her access to the Treasure Tablet before the press conference. Dr. Grassley and Dr. Abdulin were, understandably, wary of Jake's participation. Vivian pulled them aside. It took some convincing, but, in the end, they agreed his involvement constituted a lesser evil than allowing Dr. Price carte blanche to loot Mirdin's tomb or whatever else he had in mind. Jake helped matters, explaining the terms he and Vivian had agreed to, and giving his word he had no ill intentions.

"Can you remember anything about the inscription on the Treasure Tablet which might be helpful?" Vivian asked once the archeologists had been reassured regarding Jake's reliability.

Grassley rubbed his pointed chin as he reflected on the question. "A very curious line about 'three mothers.'" He paused. "And a star, maybe?"

When he finished, Dr. Abdulin jumped in "Something about the sea. And a song."

The treasure hunter didn't sugarcoat his evaluation. "Three mothers, a star, the sea, and a song doesn't really get us anywhere. So what do we do?"

"Dr. Grassley and I have been considering how to proceed," Dr. Abdulin said, "The world's largest collection of Sogdian manuscripts is in Berlin, gathered from expeditions during the early twentieth century."

"It seems to us," Grassley picked up where his colleague left off, "If anyplace is in possession of information that duplicates the Treasure Tablet or provides other useful insights, it's there."

Online, the archeologists had found an abstract of the Berlin collection, itself published in the 1920s, summarizing

79

each manuscript and providing a master index of key terms and proper nouns appearing within the collection.

Scanning the index, Vivian found that the word "Mirdin," transliterated exactly as in the stele, occurred in three manuscripts. According to the abstract, Manuscript Six dealt with religion, Manuscript 17 chronicled events in the kingdom, and Manuscript 24, potentially the motherlode, recorded Mirdin's life and travels. Each was described as trilingual. Vivian hoped this included the now familiar Latin-scripted Common Brittonic.

"I don't suppose the full text or images of the manuscripts are available online?" Vivian knew the answer to the question before she asked it.

Dr. Grassley smiled apologetically, "My dear, you of all people know how little money most institutions have for digitization. And these manuscripts must rank near the bottom of a very long list of priorities."

Jake looked at Vivian, "So, I guess you and I are going to Berlin."

Chapter Fourteen

Returning to the land between the two rivers, Myrddin again marveled at the ruins of some of humanity's oldest cities. Sheltering from the summer heat, he ate and drank in the shadow of a great temple, its series of ever-smaller stories stacked atop one another. As wind whistled through the vacant streets, the weight of time pressed down heavily. These buildings had been abandoned for millennia. Even the city's ghosts had grown old and died.

The towns of the living dotted the vast distances between ruined cities of the dead. Like many of the Sogdians, this land's inhabitants were Mazdayasna. They spoke a language similar to Sogdian and he communicated with them easily. It provided a welcome reminder of the home he had departed recently. And, if dusty memory served, the locals' tongue was even more like that of Palamedes and his family than Sogdian.

The Mazdayasna ways were not his ways. But he appreciated their pageantry and dramatic aesthetic, especially their temples of sacred fire. Even after two decades among them, though, the Celt in Myrddin still shuddered at their Towers of Silence. Within, carrion birds consumed the Mazdayasna's pious dead so that their decay would not pollute the sacred elements.

The people between the two rivers claimed the ruined cities had been built by giants. The Celts said the same thing of the standing stones scattered throughout their lands. Myrddin found such sentiments understandable but, he reflected, people underestimated their ancestors' cleverness. Anyway, this was not giant country. Fairies were another matter entirely. The abandoned temples, tombs, and lonely mounds of ruins made this a perfect place for fey if he had ever seen one. In Britain or Sogdia, he need not have worried. Here, the gentle folk didn't know him. He kept careful watch from the corners of his eyes for fairies bent on mischief.

He had been traveling for six weeks. The Tarkuns, both father and son, had made great fuss over his departure.

81

Outside the house where Myrddin dwelled so many years, the elder Tarkun ordered a stone monument raised in his honor. As a special tribute, at insistence of the younger Tarkun, in addition to the twin alphabets of Sogdia, its inscriptions included Myrddin's native tongue. It struck Myrddin as terribly unnecessary. In a few generations, who could read it? Indeed, who would know who Myrddin had been? Who would care?

The elder Tarkun provided him a royal escort, with great pageantry and fanfare, to Sogdia's border. In cities, small towns, and villages, people came out to enjoy the unexpected parade and take a last look at the strange man who had dwelled among them.

Leaving the rugged, broken landscapes of Sogdia and its neighbors behind, Myrddin entered this endless sea of sand. And a sea it was, complete with both storms and waves. The waves moved with ponderous slowness, but moved nonetheless. Though the bulk of his journey remained ahead of him, Myrddin swore that sometimes he already smelled the sea, the morning mist, the plants and flowers of home.

He missed the smiling faces of Sogdia, especially the endlessly enthusiastic Tarkuns, the elder and younger alike. But he had only one real regret. Among all his treasures, he had forgotten to pack the bracelet, his only tangible remembrance of Nimue. Momentarily, he considered returning for it. But, once more, he caught the scent of the sea. Home was calling. And reminding him he had little time left.

Chapter Fifteen

They had no problem securing an early flight from Samarkand. Landing in Dubai, making further changes proved to be another matter entirely. Air travel's newest global hub buzzed with activity and was, apparently, filled to capacity.

Jake had a long conversation with the ticket agent. Though Vivian didn't understand Arabic, the treasure hunter's tone sounded like equal parts pleading and threatening. In the end, he secured them same-day tickets to Frankfurt and, from there, Berlin.

"How many languages do you speak?" Vivian wanted to know.

"Enough."

They touched down on an unseasonably cool and gray day. Their taxi traveled downtown through Berlin's wide, tree-lined boulevards. On each side, they were flanked by the city's distinct architectural hodgepodge. Bold experiments in modernism rose alongside stately old imperial edifices from the days of the Hohenzollerns. The Ethnological Museum of Berlin, formerly the Royal Museum for Ethnography, proved to be one of the latter. A long, artful rectangle flanked by Doric columns and elegant cornices, the building gave a Prussian nod to the architecture of classical Greece, accented with walls painted a delicate shade of royal yellow.

They were met by the museum's assistant curator. After introductions, she escorted them through dimly-lit tunnels lined by shelves filled with ancient boxes. If this was a movie, Vivian thought, there would be a chase scene here. She and Jake settled in to a sparely furnished research room deep in the institution's expansive subbasement, harshly lit by florescent lights. The curator then disappeared into deep storage, pulling one manuscript box at a time for Vivian and Jake to examine.

Manuscript Six recorded a religious debate at the Sogdian royal court, conducted by King Tarkun himself. Its participants were the enigmatic Mirdin and the head of

Sogdia's Nestorian Church. As the abstract indicated, the document transliterated Mirdin's name precisely as on the stele.

Two topics were debated on that long ago day. First was a question as old as time, whether concepts like goodness, balance, and justice had any independent existence outside of divine law. Vivian could not suppress a grin. Had there ever been a freshman philosophy class where that question hadn't come up? That it was already being pontificated a millennia and half ago amused her greatly. Both debaters answered similarly, somewhat sidestepping the question by saying that, of course, the divine world would be in harmony with such fundamental concepts.

Afterward, Tarkun put forth a more contentious question, whether monotheism or polytheism offered any intrinsic advantages over the other in promoting virtue. Both participants answered in the affirmative, advocating strongly in favor of their own belief. But, as she read, Vivian barely noted their specific points, focusing instead on other aspects of the document. Calling this section revolutionary was an understatement. In arguing for his polytheism, Mirdin named deities which, even transliterated, were clearly Celtic gods and goddesses like Bel, Brighid, Cernunnos, Lugh, and the Morrigan. More than that, he discussed spirituality as it related to virtue at court of the Great King Arturus. Inconsistent in its transliteration, the document named said court as "Camalod" or "Camalot."

Vivian could now confidently connect Mirdin with Myrddin. A historical Merlin, the possibility of whose existence she had refuted just days earlier, now stared her in the face.

After Manuscript Six, perusing Manuscript 17 proved an anticlimax for yielding new insights about Myrddin. Still, Vivian found the color and background it offered very interesting. Proclaiming itself an "Annual Chronicle" of the Sogdian Kingdom, it opened a window into daily of life of sixth century Central Asia. A new royal princess had been born to great fanfare and celebration. Following his venerable predecessor's demise, a new Nestorian bishop had been appointed in Kesh. A new fortress was completed in the Zeravshan Valley. Nomadic horsemen were, again, making trouble along the kingdom's northern edge.

The manuscript gave more detail to the arrival of an envoy from the neighboring King of Bactria, who believed a Sogdian trader had cheated him out of sixty talents of silver. Tarkun gave the envoy thirty. The latter promptly departed, satisfied, to his king's court. Tarkun summoned said trader to the Sogdian court for a "discussion." Vivian wondered how that went for him.

Developments in the Sogdian quarters of three Chinese cities, Dunhuang, Mogao, and Anxi, were also chronicled. Notably, a fire in Anxi's Sogdian quarter had created great hardship for its merchants. Tarkun dispatched gold and supplies to speed rebuilding, a loan to be repaid "when prosperity returned."

The chronicle recorded tallies from the year's grain and fruit harvests as well as the numbers of livestock born in each of the kingdom's provinces.

The manuscript ended with the entry: "Placed at the conclusion of the chronicle, because Great King Tarkun wishes it were not so." It noted the departure of Mirdin, the kingdom's grand vizier. Now an old man, Mirdin had departed to "bury his bones and his treasure in the land of his birth."

That only restated information available from the stele and Treasure Tablet, but lacked the descriptive language regarding Mirdin's destination which the tablet contained.

The manuscript held a mystery, however. The segment written in Roman-scripted Brittonic was much smaller than the Sogdian part. Vivian thought it unlikely the former contained all the information of the latter. Perhaps the additional bits of Sogdian concealed useful information. She emailed photos to Dr. Grassley. If anything useful lurked in the Sogdian text, he and Dr. Abdulin would find it.

Before fetching Manuscript 24 from storage, the curator was apologetic. "If memory serves, that box was heavily damaged in the war."

She didn't exaggerate. The surviving manuscript fragments were blackened nearly beyond recognition. Only occasionally could Vivian guess at a word or syllable. Anything larger, like a clause or sentence, proved beyond hope. Vivian wondered what use there could be in preserving these sad remnants. Beyond frustration, something else troubled her. "When you told us about Manuscript 24, you said 'If memory served,'" she quizzed the curator. "I doubt Sogdian inscriptions from a century-old excavation fly off the shelves. Someone's requested these records recently, haven't they?"

"Yes."

"Who?"

"Dr. Cuinnsey, you know that would be a violation of patron confidentiality."

Vivian figured German civil servants willing to accept a bribe were rare as hen's teeth. Jake got lucky. A one hundred Euro outlay from him confirmed what they both suspected, Dr. Adrian Price had examined the collection just months earlier.

Departing the museum, Vivian's curious mix of elation and disappointment began fading, replaced by fatigue and hunger. It had been a long, intense day and she'd eaten nothing since the flight from Dubai. "Jake, are you hungry?"

"I could eat."

On his recommendation, the pair found themselves at Café Buchwald, one of Berlin's venerable café bakeries. Its antique furniture, decorative wall-paper, and floral-print curtains imbued the café with the relaxed elegance of sitting room from the turn of the last century.

"Take another slice of baumkuchen, Doc," he invited her. The café's specialty, a layered chocolate and apricot cake cooked over open flame, tasted magnificent. But the flavors were too strong and rich for her to imagine ever wanting more than one slice at a sitting. Instead, she sipped her cappuccino.

Jake set down his empty cup. "So, how did you get here?"

"What do you mean?"

"I mean, did you always want to be a professor of Celtic

86

languages?"

"When I was really young, the two things I wanted to be…" she began, "One was a paleontologist. I loved dinosaurs. Still do. And a princess. I could never make up my mind which I wanted more. So I decided to become a paleontologist-princess."

As the treasure hunter laughed, she protested it was the truth. "But, as far as the road to what I actually became…you know how they say a talent for languages goes along with talents for math and music?"

Jake nodded.

"Lies. Lies and fabrications. At least for me. I'm fine with math, nothing special. Pretty good with puzzles. Crosswords, Sudoku, things like that. Music, well, I was in orchestra in Middle School. Played the violin. By the end of my first semester, our conductor, Mrs. Affolter, practically pleaded with my parents to find me another elective. My father didn't like that. Not at all. But he eventually consented."

Vivian paused, pondering where her story truly began. "I suppose it started with my grandparents. My dad has lived in the states most of his life. But we spent our summers with his parents on the Isle of Man. Sometimes Christmas, too. One summer day, I guess I was about eight or nine, I wandered away from my grandparents' house and down the hill to the village.

"Some of the old men from the village spotted me. One of them went to tell my parents where I was. To keep me occupied until they got there, the others taught me words in Manx. I remember them laughing at my accent."

Seeing Jake raise an eyebrow, she clarified, "Not in a mean way. It was good-natured laughter. Of course, this predated the Manx language revival. Most people didn't know much Manx to pass on back then. But I didn't know that at the time. Even if I had, I wouldn't have cared. It was a revelation for me.

"Before that, of course, I knew there were other languages. But until those men started teaching me one, I didn't grasp what that really meant. That an entirely other way to talk about the world existed. It was like a secret thing was revealed to me. A magic thing.

"And, Jake, I was good. In the half hour before my parents came to collect me, I mastered pretty much all the Manx those men had to throw at me. Mom and dad were furious at me for wandering off. And they almost dismissed my governess for allowing me to get away. But, eventually they noticed how much I'd learned. And they were impressed. Grandfather was even more impressed. He knew rather more Manx than the villagers. In the evenings, if I had behaved that day, he'd spend a few minutes teaching me.

"I especially came to treasure my Christmastime visits. Most nights, Grandfather and I would sit together by the fire and he'd teach me for an hour or more. That's how I developed my love of languages and, especially, Celtic languages."

The treasure hunter nodded thoughtfully as Vivian completed her story.

"Now, Jake, turnabout is fair play. What about you? How does one go from oil and gas to treasure hunting?"

"A lot of people ask me that." Jake paused. "What most of them don't get to hear is that, really, it was the other way around. The treasure hunting was my first love."

"Oh?"

"Actually, like you, I guess I owe it to my grandparents. They had this ranch, about half an hour outside this nothing little town between Lubbock and Amarillo. The real middle of nowhere. But the family gathered there for holidays. When I was six years old, after Easter supper my cousins and I went outside to play in the back pasture. We were playing tag. I looked down, and I saw an arrowhead sticking halfway out of the earth.

"Projectile point, not arrowhead." Jake corrected himself with the proper archeological term before Vivian could. It irked her that treasure hunter had anticipated her. He continued, "But I was just a kid, I didn't know that. I bent down and pulled it out of the dirt and just starred. Of course, I got tagged. But I didn't care. It was the most amazing thing

I'd ever seen. Even at that age, I had some idea that someone not too different from me, other than living a long time ago, had made it by hand. And now I was holding it in my hands."

Vivian laughed. "A flint point is archeology, Jake, but hardly treasure."

"To an adult maybe, not to a kid," as he recounted the tale, Jake's wide grin and bright eyes gave Vivian a momentary glimpse of the child he had been. "The day after we got home, I made my parents take me to the library. I checked out a book on arrowheads." He winked at her as he used the colloquial term. "I read everything I could about them. What I'd found was a Clovis point. The Clovis People were the most skilled projectile point makers the world has ever seen. The one I'd found was over 10,000 years old. Erosion must have brought the point to the surface. So, it was an unusual find, actually.

"If I wanted to psychoanalyze myself," Jake continued, "I might say all my other treasuring hunting is just an attempt to recapture the wonder I felt when I found that arrowhead."

"And what became of this first great treasure of yours?" Vivian wanted to know.

"Oh, I keep it close to my heart," Jake said. He unbuttoned his shirt's top button and pulled out a pendant on a knotted cord. On closer examination, rather than a pendant, Vivian saw a half-dollar-sized sliver of orange-brown flint tapering to a wicked point. Replacing the arrowhead and buttoning his shirt, Jake returned his attention to Vivian.

Roused by a waiter from their storytelling, they noted the café closing. In many places, so long as they didn't order anything else, casually lingering another quarter hour before leaving would be acceptable behavior. Germany was not one of those places. Out on Bartingallee, the pair hailed a cab.

Returning to their hotel, Vivian was shocked to be confronted by two Polizei investigators. "Jake Booker, Vivian Cuinnsey, you are wanted for questioning on suspicion of smuggling and violating the Antiquities Act. You will please come with us to police headquarters."

Discretely, Vivian slipped the bracelet off her wrist and

into her purse.

Chapter Sixteen

They were escorted, rather gently Vivian had to acknowledge, to a police car and driven to a very Berlin police station. The five-story nineteenth century main building had a curiously modernist extension, a three-story box with rounded corners and long panels in various hues of red, gray, and green. Once inside, the Polizei separated the two of them. The officers showed her to a small, Spartan, and brightly lit room furnished with only a desk and three chairs.

A half-hour later, two detectives entered and began aggressively questioning her. About her recent activities. About her association with Jake Booker. And, most of all, about her adherence to the 1970 *UNESCO Convention on the Means of Prohibiting the Illicit Import, Export, and Transfer of the Ownership of Cultural Property*, often shortened, for obvious reasons, to the Antiquities Act.

Vivian resented the detectives framing their questioning with an assumption of guilt. But she also noted something else. Over the years, grading papers taught her an amazing amount about the way people use language. There was a certain vocabulary and sentence structure she had come to associate with students trying to fake their way through an essay on a topic they knew nothing about. Their language was at once dramatic, verbose, and rather circular. She saw all those aspects in the detectives' questions. *They're fishing. They don't really have anything on us*. The revelation comforted Vivian. She kept her answers short, to the point, and delivered with a measured indignation.

"Look, am I being charged with anything?" she finally demanded. The detectives excused themselves.

After a quarter hour they returned and, with an antiseptic "You are free to go," escorted her to the lobby.

She found Jake sitting on a bench, sipping coffee from a paper cup and reading *Der Spiegel*. "I was wondering what happened to you."

Getting back to their room around dawn, she realized

things could have been much worse. Jake's company kept a good European law firm on retainer in Brussels. Fortunately, Dr. Grassley had completed all the required paperwork for the bracelet. Otherwise, whatever else transpired, Vivian would find herself in serious legal and professional hot water. Even as things stood, the Polizei had been very thorough.

"You know who's behind this, don't you?" Vivian asked.

"Uh-huh. Price. Obviously, he's figured out we didn't bite it in Uzbekistan. Even if the authorities didn't find anything sufficient to detain us or charge us, he probably figured it would eat up time and intimidate us."

"The real question," she reflected, "is whether he knew we were coming to Berlin to examine the Sogdian manuscripts or if it was just an educated guess."

"Actually, I think the real question is where we go from here. I'm not feeling intimidated. How about you?"

Vivian shook her head. "But, you're right, what now? Dr. Grassley responded to my email. There's nothing else useful in Manuscript 17. And he says other collections of Sogdian manuscripts are scattered all over the world and much smaller than the Berlin collection. Without the Treasure Tablet, Myrddin's trail is cold. How do we pick it up again?"

Jake scratched his head. "So." He paused. "I have a vague memory from my time at Oxford of a Victorian monograph claiming, after Camelot, Merlin traveled the world and was behind a lot of legends about wandering sages."

"Your time at Oxford?"

"Yeah, I did the whole Rhodes Scholar thing." When Vivian's expression communicated that his answer was insufficient, he continued. "I'm a pragmatist. Going to college, I was all about studying something that could land me a good job right out of school. I attended the state university near where I grew up, majoring in petroleum geology and minoring in business. But that didn't mean I wasn't curious about life's bigger questions. After establishing myself a bit, I applied for Rhodes and spent a couple years studying history at Oxford before getting back to the oil patch."

"I genuinely don't know what to say to that," Vivian

replied. "But, please, tell me more about this monograph?"

Jake searched online. With a satisfied chuckle, he motioned for Vivian to look at his tablet. "Here it is, Herbert Price," Jake said. He had located a chapter about the man in an anthology of biographies of unusual and unconventional Victorians. Together, they absorbed the text.

Herbert Price, who studied at Oxford in the mid-nineteenth century and lectured there for several years, had also been a Welsh nationalist and an eccentric. The idea of a historical Merlin who traveled the world after the fall of Camelot became an obsession for him. When that obsession began interfering with his lectures, Price was asked to leave Oxford.

The only child of a prominent Swansea physician, Price used family money to fund his efforts tracking down alleged accounts of Merlin's travels. In 1899, he self-published a monograph summarizing his findings.

Eventually dismissed as a crank and having exhausted the family fortune, Price returned to Wales and died in poverty and obscurity.

For a time, Price was friends with Sir James Frazer. Much of the data Price collected allegedly found its way into Frazer's *Golden Bough,* one of cultural anthropology's foundational texts. The two men ultimately broke over increasingly heated disagreements regarding whether kernels of truth existed at the heart of Arthurian, or any other, mythology.

Among his many eccentricities, Price argued passionately and exclusively for the Welsh origins of Merlin, becoming enraged and even ending friendships when presented with other positions.

"We should get our hands on his monograph," Jake said, "Maybe there's something we can use."

Vivian shook her head, "You're not seeing it, are you?"

"What?"

"Price. Herbert Price. Adrian Price."

Jake slapped his palm against his forehead, a gesture from a thousand cartoons brought to life.

The biography of Dr. Adrian Price on his university's

website confirmed Vivian's suspicion. "He is the great-grandson," it read, "of noted scholar Herbert Price."

While examining Price's faculty page, they took a moment to peruse his curriculum vitae, or CV, the ponderously long and elaborate version of a résumé used by academia.

Following in his ancestor's footsteps, Adrian Price's academic career began with studying history at Oxford. He supplemented history with extensive work in archeology, later taking a master's degree focused on East Asian archeology. He spent two years writing papers and participating in various excavations throughout China and Mongolia. A curious gap followed in Price's CV, during which he appeared not to be excavating, teaching, or writing.

Reappearing a year and a half later, Price secured his doctorate in archeology, this time focused on Central Asia. The pair skimmed his post-doctoral publication credits and excavation history. Vivian saw patterns. From the latest Greco-Bactrian discoveries, to the massive Kazakhstan geoglyphs, to the enigmatic Tarim mummies of western China, whenever something unusual cropped up in Central Asia, especially if it hinted at outside influence, Price was either involved from the start or got in is as quickly as he could.

"The bastard knew exactly what he was looking for," Jake concluded.

"For more than a decade, at least," Vivian agreed, adding, "and I'd trade my tenure to know what he was doing during that missing eighteen months."

When Adrian Price's online biography yielded no further secrets, they returned their attention to the elder Price. Unsurprisingly, Herbert Price's obscure monograph was not available online. A call to Oxford's Bodleian library, where someone had fortunately arrived early to work, secured a promise to scan and email the document as quickly as possible. As they waited, Vivian and Jake grabbed a few hours of badly needed sleep.

Before drifting to sleep, she looked over at Jake's bed. Since the early moments of her association with the treasure hunter, something had puzzled her. "The whole roughneck bumpkin thing you play up, it's not really you. Why stick with it?"

Jake laughed. "A lot of times it pays to be underestimated."

When they woke later that morning, an email from Oxford was waiting for them with a scanned copy of Price's monograph attached. The email added that the Bodleian's collection also possessed of a number of other documents and items connected with Herbert Price's life and travels. Apologetically, it explained the impracticality of scanning them.

Over coffee, they read.

The monograph was written in the thick, ponderous, and grandiloquent style Vivian associated with Victorian academic prose. Even that, however, could not obscure the undercurrent of feverish obsession running throughout the text. As Jake had recalled, Price hypothesized that Merlin traveled widely throughout the known world after Camelot's fall. The monograph used the Anglicized "Merlin" rather than the Celtic "Myrddin." Drawing on a variety of obscure and questionable sources, the author attempted to piece together a chronology of Merlin's wanderings.

Price believed that Merlin first traveled to Gaul, alleging he met with the ancestors of Charlemagne. He then traveled to the lands of the Gothic tribes before turning southward to Rome.

From the Eternal City, Merlin sailed to Alexandria where, Price claimed, evidence showed he spent a full year among its scholars and sages. Braving a crossing of the Sahara, he reached the city states of the Niger River. Price speculated about links between Merlin's arrival and certain stories of Anansi, the West African trickster god. Making his way to the headwaters of the Niger River and beyond, Merlin came to Axum in present day Ethiopia.

He crossed the Red Sea into Yemen and wandered up the Arabian coast, through Irem, Mecca, Jerusalem, and into

Constantinople. Price tied Merlin to pre-Islamic Arabian legends of a wizardly battle among the pillars of Irem. He also cited obscure folklore suggesting Merlin carved the true story of the Grail Quest into the wall of a cave which had belonged to Joseph of Arimathea.

In Constantinople, Price linked Merlin to records of an audience between the Orthodox Patriarch, and possibly the Emperor Justinian himself, with an unnamed "wise man of the pagan west." Thence, Merlin went southeast through Mesopotamia to the mouths of the Tigris and Euphrates. He sailed the monsoon winds to India. Traveling through the subcontinent's jungles and mountains, Merlin reached Sui China and the Pacific. Price claimed the Sui Emperor's court records showed Merlin eventually turned back westward, traveling along the Silk Road.

The monograph concluded with acknowledgement that no further records existed which Price could confidently connect with Merlin. He hypothesized that, somewhere between China and Constantinople, Merlin either settled down or passed away. If, Price noted, Merlin's final resting place could ever be found, it would be the archeological find of the century, "a discovery to eclipse Schliemann's Troy or Sir Arthur Evans' Knossos."

It intrigued and surprised Vivian that Herbert Price, apparently, never actively searched for Merlin's tomb. On the other hand, "between China and Constantinople" was a very big target and, at the time Price wrote, a largely unknown and often risky one.

The document featured extensive end-notes, including excerpts from many of the sources Price used to piece together Merlin's alleged travels. Vivian was annoyed that, in accordance with the scholarly conventions of his day, Price rendered most of these in their original language.

"What do you think?" Jake asked when they had finished. "I think he sounds crazier than an oilfield rat."

"No question the man was obsessed, quite possibly crazy." Vivian sighed. Part of her still recoiled at what she was about to say, "But Myrddin, or someone so like him as to make no difference, was in Central Asia. I think we need to treat anything in the monograph as at least possible. The question is, what does that give us?"

"It's all well and good to read the monograph. But I think the devil will be in the details."

"You're thinking about his materials at Oxford."

The treasure hunter nodded.

"Me, too. But can we afford the time to go to England and look?" Vivian paused. "More importantly, can we afford not to?"

Putting their heads together, they weighed pros and cons, deciding the consequences of making the wrong decision based on limited information exceeded those of taking extra time to get the whole picture. Securing last minute economy seats on a flight from Berlin to London, Vivian and Jake rushed to the airport.

Chapter Seventeen

Myrddin had heard the high passes of the Cappadocian Mountains were treacherous. Now he had proof. Making his way to Constantinople, bandits ambushed his little party of Byzantine traders and pilgrims. Myrddin had seen the villains' kind in half the places he'd visited, more hungry than vicious. Deserving of pity, but also fear. Dead was dead, whatever the motivation.

Myrddin's strange appearance drew the bandit leader's attention. The sole impressive specimen among the assailants, the man towered over him, very nearly a giant. Perhaps giantish blood flowed in his veins. Raising his appropriately proportioned sword, the bandit brought it down on him, slamming into the shield Myrddin had carried for two decades. While he had kept it for sentimental reasons, that did not mean he refrained from using it when circumstances required.

As the shield's hardened camel hide took the blow, the sword shattered upon contact with it protective covering of iron studs in shape of a Nestorian Cross. That did not surprise Myrddin. Large, cheap weapons often proved brittle as well. The visual effect was nonetheless impressive.

No one but his outsized opponent saw Myrddin break an eggshell across the giant's neck and chest. The others only heard Myrddin's angry chanting and witnessed the giant screaming in pain, clawing at his own flesh as multi-hued vapors began swirling at the wizard's feet.

The image must have been striking indeed. The bandits turned tail and retreated into the mountains from which they came.

Reaching the nearest town, Myrddin again discovered no good deed remained unpunished. More superstitious than the Sogdians, several of the Byzantines in his traveling party had whispered tales of black magic to the local priest. The cleric seemed insufficiently willing to wait for proof of Myrddin's claims of friendship with Justinian. And, Myrddin admitted to himself, "friendship" stretched the truth. But he had hoped the emperor's name would intimidate the man.

The priest, however, let it be known he wasn't indifferent to other concerns, mentioning several of the travelers had commented upon the shield which bore the holy cross of Nestor. The shield which "miraculously" shattered the bandit chieftain's sword. Such an item, the priest intimated, would be a worthy addition to his church's relics.

Myrddin was sorely tempted to point out the absurdity of suspecting him both of witchcraft and of carrying a holy item. That seemed unlikely to help. Myrddin knew his skin was wrinkled and unlovely, but he liked it intact all the same. Delivering the shield to the priest, Myrddin reflected that it had now saved his life three times.

Continuing on the road to Constantinople, Myrddin considered complaining to Justinian about the cleric's behavior. But its original owner, he suspected, might prefer the shield to serve as an object of inspiration and reverence in a church rather than a keepsake for a crazy old pagan.

Chapter Eighteen

As it so often was, escaping Gatwick airport proved an exercise in patience that would tax Job. By the time Vivian and Jake collected their rental car, hours had bled away.

Finally underway, driving through the summertime English countryside, Vivian found it difficult to remain tense. Driving past green fields and meadows bursting with daisies, peonies, poppies, sweat peas, and sunflowers, she reflected on how little time she spent here. England, aside from academic conferences in London or research in Cornwall, was someplace she went through. To the fields and rolling hills of Wales. The harsher-edged beauty of Scotland. Or home to the Isle of Man. Places where successive waves of Saxon, Dane, and Norman invaders hadn't erased most traces of Celtic from the language and landscape.

The medieval and ultra-modern cohabitated in the old county town of Oxford. At its heart, of course, stood the university whose name had become synonymous with knowledge. Since its establishment in the eleventh century, Oxford had known few peers and no betters among the world's centers of learning.

Though she kept it to herself, it amused Vivian to see Jake in this setting. With his rustic appearance and casual demeanor, the man stood out like a sore thumb. But his obvious comfort, even familiarity, in his surroundings testified the man had spoken truthfully when he claimed kinship with the university.

Oxford's library was a monument to a millennium of scholarship. Or rather, its libraries. The university nurtured more than 120 such repositories on its grounds. But the Bodleian Library represented the crown jewel of them all, its holdings divided among two adjacent buildings. The seventeenth century "Old Bodleian" appeared equal parts cathedral and fortress. The "New Bodleian" was a 1940s creation designed with a clear nod to ancient Mesopotamia.

Jake indicated Herbert Price's material would be in the

latter, the "New Bod" as he called it. She was surprised when, with a mischievous twinkle in his eyes, he urged her through the "Old Bod's" formidable wooded doors. "We've got a little time to spare, I think. I couldn't forgive myself if you didn't have a chance to browse."

Vivian's research took her to libraries and archives around the world. Typically, such institutions required her to acquire a courtesy borrower's card, a researcher's card, or sign a document affirming she had read and understood the repository's policies. Ritual-soaked Oxford found those options too pedestrian. Known among students as the "Bodleian Initiation," accessing its collections required a sworn oath.

Standing before the Bodleian's ruddy-faced collections manager, Vivian swore she would "not remove from the library, nor to mark, deface, or injure in any way, any volume, document or other object belonging to it or in its custody. Not to bring into the library, or kindle therein, any fire or flame, and not to smoke in the library. And I promise to obey all rules of the library."

Turned loose on the Old Bod's holdings, Vivian almost believed she had died and gone to some very special heaven reserved for historians and linguists. Within the Bodleian's walls were treasures beyond counting. A *Gutenberg Bible*. A Shakespeare *First Folio*. The correspondence and personal papers of the poet Shelley. A surviving copy of the first book printed in North America. Biblical literature in Latin, Greek, and Coptic from the sixth century onward. Not one but four original copies of the *Magna Carta*. Several surviving Mesoamerican codices predating contact with Europeans. The *Ashmole Bestiary*, the beautifully illustrated twelfth century manuscript was one of the oldest surviving works of zoology. The *Vernon Manuscript*, one of the most important surviving Middle English documents. The list went on.

Two items in particular made her scholar's heart sing: Thomas Carte's priceless collection of documents related to the history of Ireland and the *Song of Roland*, an eleventh century French epic poem chronicling eighth century events, a time when France's linguistic and cultural Celtic substratum remained much thicker.

"Okay, Doc," Jake said, tugging her away from one of the items in Carte's collection. "Remember what we're here for. We can come back to the candy store later."

Vivian knew the treasure hunter was simply being prudent. That didn't prevent her from shooting him a dirty look as she, reluctantly, put the document away.

The rather officious collections manager in front of whom Vivian had sworn her oath now escorted them deeper into the library. The Bodleian, she realized, dwarfed the Ethnological Museum of Berlin. "It's huge," she whispered as they walked.

"The Old Bod and New Bod are like the tip of an iceberg," Jake commented. "The library's stacks run for miles underneath the university."

They were shown into a comfortable old-fashioned sitting room with rich, dark wooden paneling. Thick green carpet covered the floor while comfortable leather chairs surrounded a mahogany table. Along one wall, manuscript boxes filled Victorian bookshelves conspicuously matching the table. The collections manager began pulling boxes and carrying them to the table. "Let me know if you require additional assistance," he informed Vivian and Jake as he finished and exited.

That surprised her. "They're just going to leave us here, unsupervised, with all this?"

"I've got a little pull here," Jake said. "I learned a lot here. And had a lot of fun. I've been generous. Not much by Oxford standards, but enough to earn a perk a two. Besides," he added, smiling "We've both taken the oath."

Vivian began perusing the collection's *Calendar & Inventory,* the archaic term for what modern collections called the "finding aid." The brief document detailed the collection's history and provided an annotated list of its contents.

According to the history, while some of the collection's contents were already present at Oxford, the remainder arrived in 1911, after Price's death. Herbert Price, it seemed, forgot to change a key provision of his will after falling out with Oxford half a century earlier. His son, Edward Iorwerth

Price, brought suit against the university to recover Herbert's materials. The case slowly wound its way through the British legal system, ultimately being dismissed amidst the more pressing needs of the Great War.

In the 1950s, Herbert's grandson renewed the suit, until the court threw it out on a technicality. In 1994, the great-grandson, Adrian Price, formally renounced any family claims to the collection. If Vivian did her math correctly, Adrian had been 18 at the time and shortly afterward became a student at Oxford.

The first box contained items related to Herbert Price himself, mostly dating from his time at the university. Vivian found much of it of limited interest. That included several papers from his days as a student. She noted Herbert received very good marks, even if his professors often complained they found his ideas unconventional or even radical.

Notes for Price's lectures on British history comprised the majority of documents in the box. Many of them included substantial commentary on aspects of Arthurian myth and legend. The lectures confirmed, as Vivian and Jake already knew, Price's belief that significant kernels of truth existed at the heart of these legends, including the historical existence of a very Welsh Merlin. But nothing in them shed new light on Price's theory of a globetrotting Merlin or the wizard's specific origins.

Accompanying Price's lecture notes were several written reprimands from superiors for emphasizing Arthuriana at the expense of more salient and substantive elements of British history.

At the box's bottom was an old ambrotype photograph showing a group of formally posed and well-dressed students. Written at the photo's top was "Cryptothyra Society—1853." Even if the name of each person in the picture had not also been written, Vivian would have known Herbert Price. The man at the group's center was a shorter, fleshier incarnation of his great-grandson. His wild-eyed expression fit all too well with the man authoring the half-mad prose of the Merlin monograph.

Jake supplied another piece of information, exclaiming. "Hey, that's the room we're in!" And it was. Comparing the photo with the chamber she and Jake now occupied, the Cryptothyra Society had, apparently, met in the very place where the library now stored Price's collection.

As to what the Cryptothyra Society had been, that took more detective work. Searching online revealed "Cryptothyra" referred to an order of mollusks. That seemed an unlikely genesis for the society's name. It was also, Vivian realized, Greek for "Secret Door." That felt more promising. Turning the photo over, Vivian discovered a large envelope taped to its back. The papers inside shed light on her questions.

The university chartered the Cryptothyra Society in 1848. A copy of the charter proclaimed the organization "dedicated to discovering and recording the secret doors, unknown passages, and forgotten chambers within and under the university and city of Oxford." Its motto was the ominous *Et qui videt imperium*. He who sees, controls.

"Would something like that really be substantive enough to merit its own society?" Vivian asked the Oxford alumnus in the room.

"Oh yeah," Jake replied. "In a thousand years, things here have been built, rebuilt, and renovated so many times that things got lost. The city's like that, too. Below the surface, Oxford is filled with tunnels, old vaults, subbasements, access conduits, utility ducts, and who knows what else. Hell, I'm surprised they never found a Balrog.

"A lot of those places are half—or completely—forgotten now. In the Victorian Era, the city built a new sewer system but just left the old one down there disused and unmapped. There's even a subterranean river. It's rumored a lot of those places all link up, if you know how to find them."

Reading further, they learned Price had been the society's founder and, apparently, its sole president and secretary over the organization's brief history.

In 1854, the year after the photo, scandal consumed the Cryptothyra Society when two junior members disappeared exploring a tunnel under Magdalene College. In the resulting investigation, the society's member, and former members, described Price's behavior as controlling, overbearing, and secretive. Almost tyrannical. When it was shown he repeatedly failed to adhere to the club's charter, the university forced the dissolution of the society, whose membership had already dwindled to almost nothing.

The envelope's documents concluded with a written mea culpa from Price to Oxford's administration. He accepted responsibility for the boys' disappearance and admitted his failings as an officer of the society. Vivian examined it carefully, seeking clues to Herbert Price's character. Whatever else he had been, he seemed to be no monster. Unless he was a liar of exceptional caliber, Price felt genuine guilt and remorse over the disappearances.

Interesting as all that was, with great relish Vivian moved from materials about Price to the materials collected by Price.

Chapter Nineteen

He sat in the imperial courtyard, awaiting his second audience with Justinian. Fully two decades had eclipsed since the first. All around Myrddin, palace servants gathered walnuts. It was the wood that held real value. The Byzantines used sturdy, pliant walnut for shipbuilding, making sword and knife hilts for Justinian's ever-campaigning armies, and even furniture for the wealthy. But, while the trees slowly grew large enough to be worth cutting, the locals happily harvested their annual bounty.

Gathering the nuts into enormous bushel baskets, a servant occasionally cracked one open and popped the walnut's meat into his mouth as he continued harvesting. The power of certain sensations, particularly sound and smell, to conjure memories always amazed Myrddin.

He could never hear the cracking of walnuts without being transported to a long ago day in the shadow of Pendragon Castle. Myrddin was tutoring Arthur. At least, that's what Uther thought. In reality, Myrddin rested in the shade of a walnut tree, dreaming of Nimue and occasionally eating slices of the candied apple she gifted him at their most recent meeting.

Noise disrupted his thoughts. Young Arthur, still holding to the last remnants of boyhood, cracked open walnuts for a tasty snack. Myrddin sighed, Uther did not pay him to daydream.

"Bring the shells here," he instructed his pupil.

Enthusiastically, Arthur complied, bringing the halves of three walnuts he had opened.

Taking three of the walnut halves, Myrddin concealed a pebble under one. With his long, elegant fingers, he shifted them around on the ground in front of the prince. "Where is the pebble?"

When Arthur indicated a shell, Myrddin raised it, revealing the tiny stone underneath. Arthur beamed, clapping enthusiastically. They played several times more. Perception was one of Arthur's gifts. He found the pebble more often than chance alone would decree.

"If I find it again, will you give me the candied apple?" Arthur always had a sweet tooth.

"And what will you give me if you fail?" the wizard inquired.

"I don't know. What do you want?"

"Clean my clothes and blacken my boots for a week."

"Princes do not clean clothes," Arthur proclaimed with the absolute certainty of youth.

"And wizards do not dispense candied apples."

"I see your point," Arthur conceded, agreeing to Myrddin's terms.

Grinning, Myrddin put the remaining three walnut halves in play, quickly sliding the six shells around. At last, he pulled his hands away. "Now, young prince, which one is it?"

Arthur pointed to the shell on the far left. Myrddin raised it, revealing emptiness. One at a time, he lifted the other shells, all vacant. From within the folds of his robe, Myrddin produced the pebble.

"Hey, you cheated!"

"Did I?" Myrddin responded. "Just because you have choices doesn't mean any of them have to be right."

Arthur's brow furled as the boy turned that over in his mind.

"Okay, once more, double or nothing."

Curious to see what Arthur planned, he agreed.

Again, Myrddin shifted the six shells around. When he finished, the young man turned them over one at a time. All empty. After turning over the final shell, Arthur plucked another pebble from the ground and put it under the last shell, announcing "Just because I have choices, doesn't mean all of them have to be wrong, either."

That pleased Myrddin. Arthur was a quick student. "There is one more lesson for you in this," he said.

"What is that, teacher?"

"That I have only one candied apple to give," he smiled as he handed the delicacy to the boy. "But there is no doubt you earned it."

Chapter Twenty

Reaching into the next box, Vivian pulled out a written copy, presumably made by Herbert Price, of a document in Saxon. While not very familiar with the language, she knew enough that a quick glance told her this was not the Anglo-Saxon that gave rise to English. Rather, it was the old continental Saxon that influenced Low German. Notes, also presumably in Price's hand, were attached. They identified the text as part of a venerable Saxon chronicle and provided his translation.

The chronicle recounted an unusual duel between two shield maidens; Geva, a Saxon, and Hild the Brown, a Goth. According to the chronicle, the women fought as champions of their respective tribes over the ownership of a "treasure ship," a gilded, bejeweled, and allegedly magical longship.

Hild slew her opponent, forcing the chronicle to take great pains explaining how the Saxon maid had been bested by a Goth. Hild, it claimed, received aid from an "aged fiend in human form" from the land of Britons who tutored the young Goth princess in sorcery and dark trickery.

Much of the collection followed the same format as the Saxon chronicle. Price's transcription or copy of an original text was accompanied by his notes and translation into English.

Next from the box was a letter from Bishop Gainas of Alexandria to the Patriarch of Constantinople. Price discovered the missive while in Istanbul perusing the archives of the Orthodox Church.

I write Your Holiness continuing our correspondence regarding the difficulties posed by Alexandria's "learned" community. Of late, these are much exacerbated by one Myrdon, a rabble-rouser from Albion. He mocks our clergy, encourages the questioning of canon, and openly defames the church for abolishing that repository of pagan lore with which this city was once associated. I have requested that the Byzantine Prefect move against the instigator. He replies that, in light of the current religious situation in Aegypt, he will not

*make action without blessing from Your Holiness. I write,
beseeching Your Holiness to communicate such blessings.*

By "repository of pagan lore with which this city was once
associated," Gainas could only mean the Great Library of
Alexandra. Briefly, Vivian felt the wistfulness of every
historian, classicist, linguist, and bibliophile contemplating
the treasures that library once held, now lost forever. As to
"the current religious situation in Aegypt," she had no idea.
Searching online revealed that, during a brief period in 530s,
there were three competing claimants, including Gainas, to
the title of Bishop of Alexandria. A different theological and
political faction backed each man. Little wonder the prefect,
the city's civilian ruler, had not wished to move on instruction
from only one of them.

The frustration Gainas felt being snubbed by the prefect
must have been dwarfed by his frustration at the patriarch's
response, also included in Price's materials. His ecclesiastical
superior commanded the bishop not only to leave "Myrdon"
unmolested but also to inform the rabble-rouser from Albion
of an open invitation to the court of Justinian.

Vivian considered the patriarch's response. True, Emperor
Justinian was a tireless and often brutal promoter of his faith.
But he had also been a patron of learning with a powerful
desire to reassert imperial control over areas Rome had lost to
barbarian invasion. On both points, the rabble-rouser from
Albion could be a source of valuable information.

Continuing her online research, she wondered if it was
coincidence that, shortly after his exchange with the patriarch,
Gainas had fallen from Orthodox favor, spending the
remaining decades of his life in exile in Sardinia.

Not as exciting as a duel between shield maidens, Vivian
reflected. But it had value. Because Alexandria's unique
ecclesiastical situation had been a well-documented but very
temporary one, it allowed Myrddin's presence there, if it was
Myrddin, to be firmly dated to that brief moment in the mid-
to late 530s.

The same box contained another item Price procured
during his trip to Istanbul. A round shield covered with

hardened leather, now brittle with age. Though most of its iron studs had vanished, the holes left behind showed the shield had once displayed a distinctive cross, each of its arms forking into three branches at the end. A yellowed label attached to its interior proclaimed "'Wizard's Shield,' c. sixth century, Ottoman Anatolia."

The third box began with a sketch, filled in with water-colors. Commentary indicated the image reproduced a painting that Price encountered in a church in Lalibela, Ethiopia. That mountainous city, Vivian knew from some of her more unorthodox reading, was also a reputed resting place for the Ark of the Covenant. If such a thing ever existed.

The painting of figures breaking bread around a table could easily be mistaken for a portrayal of the Last Supper. Only careful examination revealed eleven people in the scene, not thirteen. And, if Price's reproduction was felicitous, the original artist had taken great pains to indicate one figure, in contrast to the others, as distinctly pale. As Price's notes indicated, that figure's clothing and full beard did not match any Caucasian group with which the priests of Aksum should have been familiar. In fact, to Vivian's eyes, they looked quite Celtic.

The following item appeared to lack an original text, consisting only of several handwritten pages by Price. Nevertheless, Vivian's eyes went wide as she scanned its first lines. Price claimed the document included excerpts from the *Al-Kitaba Manat*. Allegedly a compendium of long vanished Arabian history and geography compiled by an unknown author in the late sixth century, most scholars regarded it as myth.

Certainly, no confirmed copies existed. A handful of rumored ones were said to be in jealously guarded private collections across the globe. Sir Richard Burton, a contemporary of Price's and a fellow Oxford alumnus, claimed to have perused one. Then again, Burton claimed a lot of things. Wondering where, and how, Price accessed a copy, Vivian read onward.

111

I hope Burton's memory is so sharp as he claims. Under no circumstances will he reveal where he encountered the original. I pay a high price to access his copy, created from recollection after the fact. The man is reckless, eccentric, and obsessive; a freethinker and a deviant. Owing such a man a favor may prove a poor bargain indeed."

So, Burton had recreated the book from memory. That was useful information. While not her field, if his text could be located, it would be a reputation-making coup for somebody. Vivian smirked at Price's description of Burton, delivered without apparent irony. Short of "deviant," and, for all she knew, that too, Price might be describing himself. She continued reading Price's excerpts from Burton's text.

"Ire of the Pillars was whispered to be the gateway to (the city without a name?) and other terrible secrets of the elder world. As such, ancient ways died hard there. It was the last of Arabia's great cities to be ruled by a wizard, its sorcerous dynasty existing into living memory. Its last King, Shaddad, fell in a (magical?) duel with Mirdin al-Gharbi. Irem never recovered from the loss of her king and, soon after, the (sands?) swallowed it."

Vivian noted the text translated "Mirdin" identically to Sogdian. Jake added that "gharb" meant "west" in Arabic, making "al-Gharbi" something like "Of the West" or "The Westerner," an accurate description of the Celtic world's geographic relationship to Arabia. But what of the wizardly duel? Of course, it couldn't involve actual magic. But what did it mean? All that, of course, assumed Burton didn't make the whole thing up. Not something she'd rule out.

Next came a record from the imperial court of China's Sui Dynasty. It ordered the execution of a court official charged with giving the secrets of "fire medicine" and silk to a barbarian identified alternately as "Mei-lin Kai-er-te-rin" or the "Mei-lin Gui."

As a linguist, Vivian did not need to read Price's notes to recognize "Kai-er-te-rin" as a rough cognate with "Celt." As for "Gui," she was uncertain. So, it turned out, was Price. Fortunately, she had resources Herbert Price never dreamed of. Using her phone to photograph the ideograms Price had copied, she sent the picture to a colleague in her university's Asian Language department.

The order of execution concluded with notice that the Sui Emperor had dispatched riders toward the setting sun in hopes of catching "the Gui" before he "reached the barbarian kingdoms where the emperor's decrees carry no writ."

Vivian's phone buzzed with an incoming email from her colleague. The inscription was Middle Chinese, he informed her. In modern Mandarin, which evolved from Middle Chinese, "gui" meant ghost or demon. It was also a less than flattering term for foreigner, similar to the better known Cantonese "gweilo." But her colleague could not state with certainty whether gui carried that connotation in Middle Chinese as well.

A bigger bombshell came from the colleague's observation that "fire medicine" was the literal translation of the Chinese word for gunpowder. If it meant the same thing in the Middle Chinese of the sixth century, the date for gunpowder's invention would need to be pushed back almost two centuries.

The following bundle, bound together with twine, proved thicker than the previous ones. It began with an 1837 issue of the *Journal of the Asiatic Society*. Scrawled notes in the margin indicated which article had drawn Price's attention. Its author, James Prinsep, was described as a British East India Company official who supervised the company's mints in Delhi and Varanasi. Unsurprisingly, Prinsep had been an enthusiastic numismatist who possessed a keen interest in the history of India's indigenous coinage.

His article, "The Curious Question of Brythonic Coinage on the Subcontinent" reported on a number of Briton and Romano-Briton coins found in India. While some had been discovered only recently, others had been part of princely curiosity cabinets for centuries. Based on dates and inscriptions from the coins, they came to India either during a single incident in the sixth century or over a span of time in the fifth and sixth centuries.

Prinsep's meticulous article indexed all known examples of the coins, indicating their current owners and locations as well as the dates and circumstances of discovery, if known. The article included a map plotting locations of the coins' discovery: Goa, Hyderabad, Raipur, Jamshedpur, Kolkata, Darjeeling, Itanagar, and Ledo. Even had Prinsep not pointed it out, any observer could see the locations formed a line between India's western coast and its eastern borders with Southeast Asia and China. As he noted, geography argued the coins' movement was from west to east.

Wondering if Price missed the significance, Vivian noted a curious footnote in Prinsep's text, acknowledging "reports of similar coins from the Khanates of Bokhara and Samarqand." Old spellings for Bukhara and Samarkand, regions once at the heart of Sogdia.

Other papers in the bundle showed that, half a century after Prinsep's article, Herbert Price corresponded with several Anglo-Indian numismatists as well as the then owners of many coins identified in the article. He followed this with an 1889 voyage to India during which he acquired some of the coins referenced in his correspondence. Price's account of his trip began:

Not since Merlin's time in Alexandria can I imagine him wishing to tarry so long in a single location. No doubt the Hindoo's fakirs and yogis interested him greatly.

A brief scan of his journal suggested not all of Price's acquisitions came legitimately. He risked life and limb to obtain several through chicanery or outright theft.

Behind the journal and Price's papers, she found a dried and cracked leather pouch. Shaking it gently, the sound of metal striking against metal issued from within.

"Could it be?" Vivian turned the pouch upside down. A dozen coins fell out, making a pleasing plunk as they struck the wooden table.

Gold and silver gleamed in the electric light. The coins' irregular shape, rough minting, and weathered faces gave them a savage beauty; so unlike the uniform precision of modern currency. A gold aureus landed on its edge and

114

spiraled inward, making the unmistakable noise of a coin rolling across a hard surface, before falling flat.

Vivian intuited something. What she had in her purse, in her bank account, was *money.* This was *treasure.* They were totally different things. She suspected the covetous glint in her companion's eyes was matched by one in her own. For a moment, Vivian had a very good window into Jake Booker's mind.

When the moment passed, Vivian returned the treasure to its pouch.

When they found the real treasure, however, it proved to be of paper and ink rather than gold and silver. Once they had their hands on it, it took them awhile to realize it.

Chapter Twenty One

Jake spotted it for what it was. She had taken it for a simple editing proof of the conclusion to Price's monograph. Wanting to be certain, Jake gave it a thorough read through, comparing it to the text of Price's monograph on his tablet. Rather than an editing proof, it preserved an earlier, and significantly different, draft of the conclusion.

In this version, Price noted two accounts, each from about 30 years after the Sui Empire records, fitting the pattern of earlier Merlin stories. These accounts, one from Constantinople and the other from the Merovingians, led him to speculate Merlin had indeed settled along the Silk Road ... before returning to Western Europe toward the end of his life. Clearly, Price later developed enough skepticism to exclude this idea from the monograph. But not enough skepticism to throw the earlier draft away.

Included with that early draft was the Merovingian source Price referenced. It came from the obscure *Life of St. Radegund*, a sixth century Frankish princess of such piety that the independent-minded and progressive Merovingians made her a deaconess, a priest in all but name. Before her canonization, Radegund established the Abby of Sainte-Croix in Poitiers.

Like the *Al-Kitaba Manat*, no surviving copies of the saint's biography were known to exist. Some sources claimed the monks of Sainte-Croix kept a secret copy at their library, fearful to let outsiders see a document that likely painted their patroness with more than a trace of Catharism.

Price's translation recorded a meeting between St. Radegund, accompanied by an aged friar identified only as Frère L'Ancel, with an ancient traveling holy man of the Brittonic People. Remembering the parable of the Good Samaritan, Radegund fed and lodged the traveler. In gratitude, her shared with her secret knowledge of Joseph of Arimathea and Christ he had acquired while traveling in the Holy Land.

In turn, she absolved the holy man of an unspecified mortal sin.

Returning to Celtic lands from points further eastward, Vivian reflected, Poitiers would be a very natural stop.

While Price had, ultimately, kept it out of his monograph, that he had even briefly entertained the idea of Myrddin returning to the **west** made it all the more surprising he never actively sought Myrddin's final resting place. Perhaps he did and records of it were not here. But, if he had looked, he had not found it. At least, no evidence existed of such. And it was very telling that his great-grandson clearly believed he had not.

"That's everything?" Vivian asked.

"That's it," Jake replied, turning the final box upside down to demonstrate the point.

That didn't sit right with her. When every item constituted a revelation, it was easy to overlook that there had not been many items. Certainly not enough to account for every aspect of Myrddin's travels as alleged by Herbert Price. Vivian again reached for the *Calendar & Inventory*. As she feared, several items listed on the inventory were nowhere to be found.

Where were notes related to a meeting between Theudebert, King of the Franks, and a sage fleeing the despoiling of Briton and the death of his king? That could be a goldmine. If the connection to Myrrdin was correct, what advice had he given the king? And could it be mere coincidence that Theudebert had been the antecedent of Charlemagne?

What happened to diplomatic correspondence between various Christian and Jewish kingdoms of southern Arabia pertaining to a wandering *sahir*, a wizard? That loss hurt, too. Southern Arabia remained a cornucopia of lost cities and forgotten history. Price's notes might plug some of those holes.

There was no way she and Jake could overlook two "books" of beaten sheets of bound copper, engraved in an unknown alphabet. Price acquired them during a visit to

117

French West Africa, claiming them to be seventh century texts from the Empire of Awkar recording myths and folklore.

What became of the journal detailing Price's long expedition to the Holy Land? According to the finding aid, it contained "his interactions with Ottoman officials, transcripted conversations about folklore with villagers in the Levantine Hills, and sketches of inscriptions from antiquity."

Where, for that matter, was Price's correspondence with Sir James Frazer? Or the minutes from the Cryptothyra Society's meetings and Price's personal journal as the society's president. Jake winced at that.

Rounding out the absent items were materials Price believed pertained to two separate meetings with Emperor Justinian, a series of photographic plates acquired from British and German archeological expeditions in Mesopotamia, and an elaborately engraved silver torc discovered during the excavation of a church destroyed during the Ostrogoths' sack of Rome in 546.

In total, she found nearly a dozen items listed on the *Calendar & Inventory* absent from the physical collection.

Jake caught something else. On the finding aid, by the entry for each missing item was a tiny checkmark, written so faintly in pencil as to be barely noticeable. Whoever took the items had practically waved the theft in the Bodleian's face.

"We need to let the library know about this," Vivian concluded.

The treasure hunter nodded. "I'll tell the collections manager. He'll love that. Besides, my legs could use a stretching. I don't think I've ever played scholar this long in a single sitting before, Doc. I don't know how you do it."

As Jake exited, Vivian returned to the *Calendar & Inventory*. She wanted to give it another going through to ensure nothing else was missing. As she worked, a hollow clack, like the sound of bolts sliding in an antique door, disturbed her. In disbelief, she watched one of the long, vertical wooden wall panels swing away from the wall. From the passageway behind, five people poured into the room.

"Dr. Cuinnsey!" Clearly, Adrian Price was as surprised and displeased to find her here as she was to see him.

"Dr. Price." Vivian didn't so much speak the words as seethe them.

Four tough-looking men formed a protective wall around the archeologist. Vivian would have bet her pension none of them could be found on Oxford's enrollment rolls.

"You're a smart woman," Price began, "I thought, on top of everything else, your troubles…in Berlin would have shown you that you're out of your depth."

"This is bigger than me. And bigger than you. History and archeology aren't your private treasures. They aren't anyone's. They're everyone's."

He regarded her with wry amusement, "Is this the part where you say 'It belongs in a museum,' and I respond that 'Coronado is dead and so are all his grandchildren?'"

It irritated Vivian that Price knew that reference. With a derisive snort, he continued. "The modern world suffers a delusion that the fruits of knowledge belong to all. The Victorians came closer to the truth. Knowledge is a privilege for those fit to find, decipher, and use it. For the elite not only of mind but of vision. Like the days of Myrddin himself, when true learning belonged only to the few like him."

"All of which is an eloquent way to say 'When I was a boy, I never learned to share. In fact, I'm still a boy.'" Vivian retorted, adding, "And you're wrong about Myrddin. If you'd paid attention to what is actually in those records, instead of just treating it like a treasure hunt, you'd notice he shared knowledge everywhere he went. For what it's worth, I'm pretty sure your great-grandfather wouldn't approve of what you're doing either. His monograph proves that. Herbert spent his life trying to convince the world of Myrddin's reality. Too bad nobody believed him."

Price flinched. While her dig about his ancestor's disapproval clearly reached him, he recovered quickly. "Lovely as it's been to chat, the rest of my great-grandfather's collection needs to be taken out of circulation, for good. After Samarkand, the world does know about Myrddin and I can't afford to leave such records where anyone can access them. Not that it matters for you. You're being taken out of circulation, too. Not permanently. At least not yet. Actually, it's fortuitous you're here. There's some help you can give me with the Treasure Tablet. Alas, I fear your charmingly rural companion won't get very far on his own."

"Now!" Price hissed, as his bodyguards fanned out toward her.

Quickly, Vivian snatched an object off the table. Then, groaning as she strained, Vivian turned the heavy mahogany table over onto its side. As she did so, it amused Vivian that she was violating the Bodleian Oath she'd taken only hours ago. But it was a lesser evil than what Price had planned. The table fell toward the others, tossing fourteen hundred years of paper, parchment, and artifacts into the air, landing in a chaotic heap on the floor. If Price sought something specific, he would have a devil of time finding it.

One of Price's men planted a hand on the edge of the overturned table, using it like a gymnast's vault to swing to other side. Vivian had not expected such speed and grace from the brute. More quickly than she could react, he inserted himself between her and the exit. He treated Vivian to a very unpleasant smile.

Vivian returned a nasty smile of her own. Turning over the leather bag she held in one hand, a stream of gold and silver coins fell to the floor. Eyes going wide with avarice, he instinctively lowered himself to collect them. Stopping midway, he glanced at Price. The archeologist shook his head. By then it was too late. The man had already disadvantaged himself.

Vivian raised her knee into his groin. As he went rigid and unresponsive, she slammed his head into the thick door. The man collapsed to the ground. Though he moaned and writhed, he clearly hovered on unconsciousness.

Another of the goons hopped the table, threatening her with a meaty fist. The five gaudy, outsized rings on his hand, she realized, made a very effective set of eight karat "brass" knuckles. Crouching, Vivian quickly scooped the leather shield off the ground. As she rose, the shield met his fist halfway with a pleasing crunch. Her assailant howled in pain. Vivian turned her small size into an advantage, using her lower center of gravity to rush him. Driving the shield into his stomach, he fell backward over the table, landing roughly on the floor.

Vivian ran out of creative ideas to defend herself. With the remaining bodyguards, now advancing warily after witnessing their friends' mistakes, almost upon her, she turned for the door. As she was nearly there, the door opened. Jake stood in the doorway. The collections manager followed the treasure hunter. Beholding the scene inside the room, the blustery, red-faced man looked set to have apoplexy right there. Behind him, the sight of a third man, clad in the ubiquitous dark blue of a police uniform, warmed Vivian's heart.

"Price."

"Mr. Booker."

"You just can't stand a fair fight, can you?"

"Of course not." Price admitted, almost gleefully, fleeing through the secret door from which he and as his men appeared. His bodyguards followed. One guard lagged behind, cradling had badly swollen hand as he ran. The man Vivian slammed against the door, however, was going nowhere. Especially once the policeman knelt beside him and applied handcuffs.

Without bothering to confer, Vivian and Jake rushed into the dark passageway after them.

Chapter Twenty Two

The narrow passage could barely accommodate a single person, especially while running. Lined by damp, irregularly-cut stone and capped by an arched ceiling tapering to a point, the secret corridor was clearly ancient. Giving chase, they turned through two intersections with smaller passages leading who-knew-where and bypassed a set of diminutive stone steps leading downward to a foul smelling lower level. Even mid-pursuit, Vivian couldn't completely suppress her curiosity.

After Price and his henchmen disappeared around a third turn, Vivian heard the sound of another door opening. Making the turn, she and Jake found themselves in a concrete tunnel. Obviously of much more recent construction, a disused Industrial Age conveyer belt and pneumatic tubes dominated the dimly lit space. Their adversaries continued their escape along an elevated catwalk as they gave pursuit.

Bursting through a creaky set of metal double doors, they entered a part of the Bodleian complex still in use. Bookshelves, chairs, desks, and couches filled the subterranean study space. Dozens of students, already disturbed by the sudden appearance of Price's party, stared in confusion as Jake and Vivian rushed through.

Further ahead, Price's henchmen placed obstacles in their path, overturning chairs and tables and tossing stacks of books from the shelves. As Vivian and Jake dodged and jumped the obstacles, Price and company increased their lead, but not enough to shake pursuit.

They followed their quarry several flights up a stairwell before emerging onto the ground floor of a building where reference books and bound periodicals lined tall shelves. Far above them was a cavernous rotunda. "Radcliffe Camera," she thought Jake said as they ran. With freedom close at hand, Price and his party poured on the speed, rushing toward the wooden doors leading outside.

Sprinting madly, Jake launched into a flying tackle, taking out the henchman with the busted hand, who still trailed his fellows. The treasure hunter was none to gentle with his takedown. Vivian expected the man would still be there when the police officer caught up.

Vivian and Jake exited Radcliffe Camera in time to witness Price and his two remaining henchman speeding away on scooters. The vehicles, she noted, had wireframe baskets the perfect size for carrying off a manuscripts box. Two other scooters, no doubt for the men now incapacitated inside, idled nearby.

Exchanging glances, Vivian and Jake climbed onto the scooters and continued pursuit. Initially, Vivian wondered why scooters and not motorcycles. She soon understood. Motorcycles would have killed them all. Oxford was an unpredictable and seemingly endless honeycomb of streets, pedestrian walkways, narrow passages, and tunnels connecting courtyards, grand buildings, and open greens. As they dodged monuments, benches, hedges, the occasional food truck, and other hazards, students scattered in every direction, frequently calling curses after them.

As an undergrad, she'd owned a Vespa. This was nothing like that. Vivian doubted she ever broke 40 miles an hour on their chase through Oxford, even in straightaways. But, in its way, this terrified and thrilled her more than flying 200 miles an hour in a helicopter over the Uzbek landscape. *Damn, was that really just days ago?* No joyride or merry chase, Vivian had to be constantly alert. Taking one turn not quite tightly enough, a stone gargoyle nearly removed her face.

Even amidst furious pursuit, her companion could not resist playing tour guide, periodically indicating points of interest. Over the noise, his comments were mostly unintelligible. Occasionally, Vivian picked out things like "That's All Souls College" or, once, something about the "headless ghost of Charles the First."

As they sped from one courtyard to another, the passageway unexpectedly doubled back on itself. One of Price's henchmen didn't make the turn. His scooter glanced off the far wall, sending vehicle and rider crashing into a stone urn. She and Jake shot by, swerving to avoid the collision. Glancing at her side mirror, Vivian saw the henchman moving. He lived. But if he didn't have a hospital stay ahead of him, she would be surprised.

Jake Booker had fine reflexes. She had seen that time and again. But he was clearly unfamiliar with scooters. In the tight turns and difficult, obstacle-strewn passages, she always led. Jake noticed, too. Pulling alongside her in a straightway, he shouted.

"Go after Price!" When she couldn't understand his next statement, Jake gestured that he would remove the remaining goon from the equation.

They accelerated, closing the distance between Price and his guard. Spotting their approach, the guard dropped back, screening his employer from their advance. Jake shot forward, swerving toward the guard. To avoid being pinned against the wall by Jake, he peeled away from Price, leaving their primary objective undefended.

The chase continued, Vivian incrementally gaining on her quarry. Price betrayed his concern with frequent glances at his side mirror.

In the end, the tiniest thing betrayed her. Turning onto a two-way street to follow Price, her mind focused on keeping the archeologist in view. Muscle memory controlled the scooter. Her very American muscle memory, unfortunately, put the scooter in the wrong lane, rapidly bearing down on a delivery lorry a score of feet away and heading right for her. Pulling hard to the left to avoid a head-on collision, Vivian lost control, sending the vehicle careening toward a kebab truck surrounded by students.

Knowing it wouldn't be enough, Vivian hit the brakes hard. Screaming and shouting, students scrambled out of her way. Hitting the kebab truck, a shower of hot chips and grilled meat flew from the vehicle. Her body, and the kebab truck, protested at the instantaneous loss of momentum.

She was dimly aware of laying on asphalt, the scooter a few feet away in front of the dented truck. One of the students knelt beside her.

"I am a fourth year Medicine student. Relax. I want to take a look at you," as the young woman spoke, Vivian felt like an observer watching it happen to someone else.

She snapped from her daze when she realized Jake stood next to the student. "What the hell are you doing?" she demanded, "Price! Go after Price!"

"Making sure you're okay is more important," he replied.

The student seemed to intuit the importance of the exchange. "If you need to carry on," she told Jake, "I am fairly confident no real harm has been done. But I will continue examining her. If I change my mind, I'll call medical services."

Jake looked at Vivian. When she nodded, he rushed to his scooter, continuing pursuit.

A few minutes later, he returned. Alone.

"Price?"

Jake scowled. "I lost him down on Broad Walk. The bastard just vanished. One moment he was there. The next he wasn't. Sorry."

Momentarily leaving Vivian's side, Jake attempted to reach terms with the food truck's owner. Their conversation proved lengthy. Rejoining Vivian, the treasure hunter's scowl remained in place.

"Everything okay?

"For what I just paid, I hope I'm part owner of that kebab truck."

Jake talked Vivian into being properly examined at one of the university hospitals. "If you're fine, we lose an hour or two. If there's something wrong and we don't know, that could get bad. This is the safe bet."

Waiting to be seen by a doctor, she inquired what became of the other henchman.

"We turned into a blind alley and I ran him into a topiary hedge. I left him in the care of some enthusiastic young men

125

with cricket bats until the police could come and collect him," Jake explained, obviously pleased with himself.

She recounted what transpired with Price before Jake's return to the reading room. Amidst the man's megalomaniacal bluster, he let slip two important things, both of them good news for Vivian and Jake. First, he was having trouble with the Treasure Tablet. That suggested they had at least some breathing room. Second, that he worried enough about Herbert Price's collection to attempt to steal the whole thing indicated it contained information that could be used to locate Myrddin's tomb. Or, at least, he feared it did.

Price had also acknowledged his responsibility for the previous thefts from the collection. But that was so predictable as to be barely worth mentioning. They suspected the minutes and journal from the Cryptothyra Society were among the first items pilfered by Price. Pilfered, and put to good use. Likely, the secret door into the room was why the society met there in the first place. As it turned out, it also ensured Adrian Price had access to his great-grandfather's materials any time he wanted.

Jake vowed, at some point, he'd return and explore the other passages they'd encountered during their subterranean chase. From the intensity in his voice, Vivian suspected Jake wanted to find the Cryptothyra Society documents as much as the missing Myrddin information. Though their conversation in Berlin already revealed it, again, it confirmed that more than just profit motivated his treasure hunting.

She made use of the downtime to email Grant. After feigning interest regarding developments in the department, she got to her real purpose, checking on Dart. The cat doted on her and didn't respond well to most other people. She hoped he was behaving himself in her absence and not making too much trouble for her good-natured assistant.

After a thorough examination, including multiple x-rays, the physician issued Vivian a clean bill of health. He admonished her to return immediately if she displayed any symptoms of concussion. Awaiting the paperwork that would clear Vivian's release, she and Jake discussed their next move.

"We've got an enormous amount of new information," she concluded. "But what does that really give us? Where does it all point?"

"There are a lot of leads from Price's collection we could follow up," Jake acknowledged. "But only one of them was, allegedly, created by Myrddin himself."

She followed Jake's train of thought. "Joseph of Arimathea's Cave in Israel," Vivian acknowledged. "That's a good point. If Myrddin really did record the story of the Grail Quest in that cave, as Herbert Price claimed, it might also provide hints about Myrddin's origins. Even if it doesn't, it's not a bad silver medal."

"I'll tell you one thing," Jake said coldly "Price is going to pay."

"For what, in particular? Trying to kill us? Stealing the Treasure Tablet? Trying to loot the Bodleian?"

"Well, yes, those." As Jake ran a hand through his shaggy, silver hair, Vivian noticed the treasure hunter's bare head. "But, sometime during that chase, I lost my hat."

Chapter Twenty Three

Dawn at his back, Myrddin gazed across the Bosporus. On its far side, Constantinople spread as far as his still keen eyes could see. He was more than halfway home. The slowly approaching coracle would carry him across the straits and into Europa.

As he waited, his eyes traveled south to the old pilgrim and trader's road. His thoughts flickered to the hollowed ram's horn he still carried. Twenty years ago, he had walked that road. He remembered it as if it was yesterday.

After Axum, where he sat with the priests in their churches hewn from living rock, he sailed across a great channel to the Hadramaut, the land once known as Sheba. That great nation had long ago splintered into petty kingdoms: Aden, Marib, Najran, Qana, Sana'a, Samharm, Shabwa, Timna, and Zafar, to name just the largest. The successor states warred with each over trade, religion, and obscure points of honor. It reminded Myrddin too much of Britain before the coming of Arthur.

As a traveling wizard, many of those kings sought to recruit Myrddin. When he refused, they encouraged him to move along. Few rulers trusted a rogue wizard within their borders. But one good thing came from his time in that land. It was there he developed his fondness for the invigorating brew made from black beans.

Sitting outside a small café in Zafar, a warm, piquant, earthy aroma filled the air. Just breathing the scent revived Myrddin's body and mind. When he inquired, the café's proprietor, aged even by Myrddin's standards, showed him a foul-looking black-brown concoction the consistency of thin stew. It boiled, bubbled, and oozed atop a brass burner heated by charcoal. Never had Myrddin beheld a beverage that would look more at home in a wizard's workshop.

Myrddin's grasp of the local language remained imperfect. If he understood the proprietor correctly, it was a stimulant, like the heated emulsions of peppermint, rosemary, or rock rose Myrddin often brewed back home. Drained by the heat and by traveling through the fractious Hadramaut, Myrddin ordered a pot of the stuff. The hot liquid burned as it flowed down his throat. Its flavor was spicy and enticing but powerfully bitter. The proprietor showed him how to add crystalized honey to cut the bitterness.

Starring at the empty pot, Myrddin thought better of the Hadramaut. Was this, after all, a land that flaunted magic openly? Peppermint, rosemary, and rock rose had nothing on the black brew. His weariness vanished as if it had never been. His mind grew alert and nimble. He conversed readily with his neighbors, confident his language skills had sharpened.

After a second pot, Myrddin felt not just refreshed but rejuvenated. In truth, he felt twenty years younger. He could take on the world. After another pot, he could take on the world ... and win. After another...

Myrddin wanted to die. The proprietor had tried to warn him. Leaving the café, Myrddin was manic. Certain, even more than usual, of his invincibility. Now, his hands shook and his stomach ached as if a sickly-sour knife stuck from it. He wondered if he would ever sleep again. His head hurt and he felt cranky.

He chased away a group of overcurious urchins by waving his staff and shouting words which, depending on his grasp of the local language, may have taught them a few things about the facts of life. Wandering through the back alleys of Zafar's bazaar, trying to walk off the concoction's effects, he'd been accosted by two would-be robbers. Myrddin yelled at them so belligerently and incoherently that they'd fled.

When sleep finally came, it resembled unconsciousness more than slumber. Before passing out, Myrddin vowed never to touch the black brew again. Next morning, he returned to the café. Only for a single pot this time. It became his daily ritual here. When he felt bold, twice a day. Never more. When Myrddin at last put the Hadramaut behind him, his camel groaned under the weight of black beans.

Traveling north with the caravans, he journeyed to Irem. The City of Pillars was the last great realm to be ruled by magic. Its wizard king reputedly knew the secret of the *Chrysopoeia*, which transmuted baser metals into gold. And, whispers said, Irem served as the gateway to secret ruins from the dawn of time.

Reaching Irem, he found King Shaddad the Tenth to be an erratic tyrant who put his subjects to death for any reason. Or none at all.

Myrddin, mostly, avoided meddling in the affairs of the lands he traveled. Occasionally, he would serve as a counselor or mentor to a remarkable individual for a time. Never more than that. But, such was the suffering of the Iremites that Myrddin abandoned that guideline.

A heredity warrior caste protected the king at all times. They would defend him to their last breath, with but a single loophole. Engraved upon the oldest and largest column in the City of Pillars, in a tongue nearly forgotten, was a commandment the King of Irem should be disposed if ever challenged and bested in duel of magic.

So it was that, at dusk on the longest day of the year, Myrddin and Shaddad faced one another amidst Irem's twenty times twenty pillars. Claiming his royal prerogative to act first, the monarch threw down a brick of silver and, with a wave of his staff and cape, transformed it to liquid.

From that single act, Myrddin understood much. Those working magic with the liquid silver took great risks. Too great, he thought. The lucky ones died suddenly. The unlucky grew troubled in their minds as their spirit consumed itself.

Shaddad challenged Myrddin to prove his power by drinking the silver. Doing so would bring inevitable, terrible death. But, to avoid forfeiting the challenge, and his life, Myrddin needed to display mastery over Shaddad's conjuration.

First admixing shavings of iron into the liquid silver, Myrddin drew his loadstone from under his robes. The loadstone was an ancient thing, nearly the size of his palm, with weathered Ogham engravings that further focused its innate magic. Waving the loadstone, Myrddin beckoned the liquid silver toward him. Slowly, it came.

Howling with outrage at being bested, King Shaddad summoned the Pillar of Fire. Never before had Myrddin witnessed one of such size and intensity. Even Bleys would have been impressed. But he knew what he must do. Approaching the dancing flames, Myrddin heard and smelled the tips of his beard singe. Without flinching, he charmed the fire. Turning it blue. Then green. He caused it to flare and burn white hot, then soothed it with song.

Spectators held their breath. King Shaddad stared, disbelieving that his magic had been so thoroughly tamed. Myrddin took the initiative. A strange-looking knife appeared in each of his hands. He whispered to the blades until, aided by arcane gestures, they floated and flew around him. The flying knifes crept forward, slowly stalking the king. Myrddin taunted Shaddad with them before attacking. Swinging his staff, the king delivered a powerful invocation forcing one knife to the ground. At the same moment, its sister blade moved in, striking Shaddad across the face and drawing much blood.

Silence resounded through the pillars. There could be no doubt that Myrddin's drawing of first blood with his enchanted knife bested King Shaddad. Adhering to their city's primordial code, Irem's warriors seized the tyrant. They stripped him of his crown, robes, and staff before turning the deposed Shaddad over to the crowd to pass judgment on him as they willed.

In gratitude, Irem's people offered Myrddin a boon of his choice. The secret of the Chrysopoeia sorely tempted him. But his love of knowledge exceeded his greed for gold. Instead, he asked to be guided to the ruins of which much was whispered in darkness but little spoken by daylight.

The following morning, Myrddin departed into the deep desert accompanied by a solitary guide. The guide's family had kept the secret of the ruins' location since time immemorial. They swore to keep their secret under pain of death, a special dispensation made for the wanderer who had overthrown Irem's tyrant.

The guide showed Myrddin the Nameless City. At last he understood why it was called that. What else could it be called? Even he dared not venture into the catacombs descending untold leagues into the earth.

Hours beyond that terrible site, Myrddin and his guide stood at the edge of a shallow saline basin stretching as far his eyes could see. This was all that remained of Quaddath, the vast inland sea where civilization flourished in previous epochs now lost to memory. He explored the scatted stones of ruined Assyrnath and Yb'b, cities raised at a time, legend said, when not everything which went on two legs was human. But, when Myrddin asked to see the Green Idol, his guide refused, shuddering as he made the sign of warding.

Once again, Myrddin joined the caravans. Forsaking Irem and its secrets, Myrddin came into the City of the Black Stone of 1,000 Gods. The jewel of the caravan routes, all wealth flowing between the Hadramaut and Constantinople passed through its walls: gold, spices, silver, amber, exotic incenses and perfumes, silk, and a hundred other treasures. There was wealth beyond counting. Yet, the city's great trading clans, jealously preserving their ancient privileges and prerogatives, horded it while many in the city knew hunger. Myrddin suspected, within a couple generations, the city would witness a much needed upheaval.

Eventually, Myrddin came into Judea. Even he was moved by the wondrous sites and history of Jerusalem. In one of the small villages beyond, he hired a shepherd, well versed in that land's hidden places, to lead him to his goal. Riding their donkeys into the northern hills, into the heart of old Arimathea, it occurred to Myrddin that the herdsman he hired as a guide was at least half crazy.

At last, the guide brought his animal to a stop. Using his shepherd's crook, he pointed to the top of a steep slope. Small caves dotted its upper reaches. A faint trail led to one cave, testament to a small but steady stream of pilgrims over half a millennia.

"Remember what I told you," the herdsman said. "Do you have the horn?"

Myrddin raised the hollow ram's horn, a *shofar* in the local tongue. The guide nodded approvingly.

Carefully, Myrddin followed the trail. Outside the pilgrimage cave, he turned around and took a deep breath. He blew the shofar. From the herdsman, he learned this was expected of all pilgrims visiting the cave, a gesture of respect for the man known as Joseph of Arimathea. The horn's deep sound bellowed through the empty valley. This pleased him. Since childhood, Myrddin loved making noise. His ritual obeisance completed, he stepped into Joseph's cave.

It was tiny, not much larger than a hut. Nostalgia briefly overwhelmed Myrddin, recalling the similarly diminutive cave where his mentor Bleys had dwelled. Not, of course, that Bleys' cave had ever been so tidy.

At the cave's far end, a niche was carved into the rock. It held a replica of the Grail. Or a replica of someone's idea of the Grail. Not close at all, Myrddin scoffed. Nevertheless, if the pilgrims were correct, the niche cradled the True Grail during the few years between the crucifixion and Joseph's journey to Britain.

Myrddin wondered what had become of the Grail. What had become of Galahad, Peredur, and Bors the Younger? Did it matter? He supposed not. He contemplated the niche and what once rested there. In hindsight, the completion of the Grail Quest had been both Camelot's high point and the beginning of the end. He wondered how the tale might have unfolded had the Grail never come to the Isles. Would Camelot and Arthur still stand? Would they have never been at all? Or would fate ensure the story remained unchanged?

Rousing himself from reverie, Myrddin noted the cave walls were covered with carved inscriptions in Hebrew, Aramaic, and Greek. Some praised the virtues of the man whose cave this had been. Others quoted from the book of the God of Rome about the last days of his Son. A few told of Joseph's other adventures, stories not previously known to Myrddin and worthy of a bard. Of course, Myrddin knew a few things of his own about the man from Arimathea and what befell the Grail upon Britain's shores. Drawing a chisel from his satchel, he took time to add them. Never lacking in confidence, he added a few lines of his own tale as well.

Myrddin turned to the cave mouth. Many days remained to reach the rock-hewn red city about which many tales were told. And Constantinople lay many days beyond that. He was curious what the curmudgeonly old churchman and his emperor would say. While Justinian's inflexible zeal counted against him, many things Myrddin heard about the young emperor led him to wonder if he would find Arthur's spirit in the man. Before descending the slope, he blew the shofar again. Delighted by the instrument's noise, he resolved to keep it.

Chapter Twenty Four

The old minivan bounced along the road. As she drove, Dr. Ella Peretz explained the area's history to Vivian and Jake. Vivian wished their host would spend more time watching the road ahead and less time looking at them.

"Arimathea is a puzzle," Dr. Peretz was saying, "Other than Christian scripture, and sources referencing scripture, no record of such a place exists. My colleagues disagree, often vehemently, whether this is because the place is entirely fictive or it is the victim of a bad transliteration."

Dr. Peretz always pronounced "colleague" as "CO-league," a linguistic tick Vivian found incredibly endearing. A decade ago, Peretz taught Near Eastern Languages at Vivian's university. After marrying, she and her husband returned to Israel where she taught at Tel Aviv University. It proved a serendipitous connection. With almost no notice, sweet Dr. Peretz dropped everything to assist Vivian with her visit. The Peretzs even put them up at their fashionable flat for the duration of their stay.

Back in England, Vivian and Jake had conducted additional research confirming Herbert Price's assertion that a cave linked with Joseph of Arimathea could be found in what was now northern Israel.

Like Myrddin, Joseph was one of history's riddles. All four books of the Gospel described him as a wealthy man who gave up the tomb he had built for himself so it could be used for the burial of Jesus after the crucifixion. The *Book of Mark* further asserted that Joseph provided the linen cloth which, if its advocates were correct, would one day be called the Shroud of Turin.

In the Middle Ages, a tradition appeared claiming Joseph had been entrusted with the Holy Grail. To ensure its safety, the Arimathean carried it Britain, then literally the edge of the known world. That, of course, brought Joseph into Arthurian legend, even if only indirectly. Accounts of Joseph bringing the Grail to Britain might predate the Middle Ages. Herbert

Price's materials certainly hinted at such. But, as yet, no earlier written source had been confirmed.

Of course, it was a valid question whether a historical Joseph, or a close equivalent, had ever existed. But Vivian was more inclined to keep an open mind on such matters than she had been a week ago.

The link between Joseph of Arimathea and the Israeli cave was new to Vivian. In some variations, Joseph actually kept the Grail in his cave for a time. While the stolen journal of Herbert Price's visit to the region might contain earlier accounts, Vivian and Jake hadn't located written evidence of the link predating the eighteenth century. While not great, it had been enough for Vivian to call her former colleague.

"In the earliest Greek copies of Luke," Dr. Peretz continued with her explanation of Arimathea's enigmatic history, "Arimathea was written with an 'h' sound at the beginning. Copies from the same period written in Syriac call it 'Ramtha.' So, scholars have claimed locations as different as Ha-Ramathaim, Ramah, and Ramallah for Arimathea."

As the minivan threaded its way into a narrow canyon, their host switched from linguistics to local history. In the first century, she explained, the canyon hosted a small colony of Essenes. The Jewish monastics had dwelled in caves high above the canyon floor. Local tradition, as Vivian and Jake already knew, connected one of those caves with Joseph of Arimathea. In Dr. Peretz's opinion, the link was more ancient than the eighteenth century.

"You know, there is an apocryphal tradition," she added, "that after the death of Jesus, Joseph renounced his wealth and became an Essene."

"There's also an apocryphal tradition that he traveled to Britain," Vivian added.

"I know," Dr. Peretz responded, "But that seems less likely, doesn't it?" Vivian and Jake exchanged looks as their host continued, "I suppose both things could be true."

"Have you been to the cave?" Jake asked.

"I have not, but one of my colleagues has. He found it very interesting. There is writing in Hebrew, Aramaic, Greek, and

Latin all over the walls. We've talked about going out and doing a proper survey."

Vivian wondered if the writing using the Latin alphabet actually recorded the Latin language. She suspected not.

Dr. Peretz parked the vehicle. A short but taxing climb up the ravine took them to the clifftop caves. A narrow, well-worn path indicated the cave they sought. Two millennia of pilgrimage had worn down the rock itself.

Inside, the cave was small. A niche incised into the far wall might once have held an ossuary, icon, or the Cup of Christ. Now it stood empty. The inscriptions mentioned by Herbert Price, and confirmed by Dr. Peretz, were nowhere to be seen. Instead, pockmarks covered the walls and shards of stone littered the cave floor.

"Someone's been here with a sledgehammer," Jake said.

Dr. Peretz was in a state of shock. "Who could have done this?"

Vivian and Jake knew.

They rode in silence back to the city. Tel Aviv always seemed out of place. Too crisp. Too sanitized. Too modern. It was as if the entire city was somehow inoculated against the enormous antiquity surrounding it in all directions.

At the Peretzs' flat, situated on the top floor of a three-story constructivist apartment building nestled in the shadow of Tel Aviv University, the trio remained somber. It horrified Dr. Peretz that someone would deface a site of historical importance and destroy its unique inscriptions. Vivian and Jake shared her outrage and, furthermore, were crestfallen their one good lead on Myrddin had been erased from existence.

By unspoken agreement, the three of them had not informed Dr. Peretz's husband of what transpired at the cave. Sensing awkwardness, Michael Peretz quickly volunteered to take their two young boys to the movies.

Similarly constrained by not sharing the true purpose of their interest in the cave with Dr. Peretz, Vivian and Jake remained silent. Vivian jumped as the ringing of Dr. Peretz's phone shattered the quiet.

Answering her phone, their host replied, "Yes, yes it is." Most of the conversation which followed took place on the other end, with Dr. Peretz frequently answering "Yes" or "I understand" as she looked increasingly unhappy. Ending the call, she regarded Vivian and the treasure hunter with trepidation. Their host obviously struggled to keep her composure.

"What is it?" Vivian wanted to know.

"Dr. Cuinnsey," she began, haltingly, "that was the dean of my department. He knew you were visiting me, I mentioned it to him after you first contacted me. He says you both are wanted for smuggling and destruction of antiquities. The Israeli Antiquities Authority and police are looking for you and the airports are being watched."

Vivian cursed. Price was using the same tactic as in Berlin, but had upped the ante.

Dr. Peretz almost lost it, "I've known you for many years. You couldn't be involved with anything like that..." She paused. "Could you?"

Vivian took her hand, "I promise we had nothing to do with vandalizing the cave. Or any smuggling or destruction."

Their host nodded, "Okay. I didn't think so." She clarified, "I couldn't believe so. But I wanted to hear you say it."

"Dr. Peretz," Jake said, in a gentle tone Vivian had not heard from him before, "I want you to think very carefully about your dean said. Did say we were 'wanted' by the authorities or did he say 'wanted for questioning' or something similar?"

"He said 'wanted.'"

It sounded like a warrant had been secured for the two of them. This was serious. Extracting themselves from this would be much more difficult and time consuming than from their brief detention in Berlin. Worse, she and Jake couldn't have much time to react. Israeli law enforcement had a reputation for many things, inefficiency was not one of them.

Vivian looked at her companion, "Jake, do you have attorneys in Israel?"

The treasure hunter shook his head, "My company doesn't have regular operations here, so I've never needed them. We could hire some, but that would take time we can't afford."

Vivian noticed Dr. Peretz regarding Jake quizzically. She had no doubt deduced the existence of a hidden agenda between her guests which she hadn't been let in on.

Her thoughts racing, Vivian asked another question, "Okay, again, try to remember the specific words your dean used. Did he only mention airports? Or did he also mention border crossings or anything like that?"

Dr. Peretz quietly replayed the conversation in her mind, "Only airports," the response sounded hesitant, "I'm mostly sure."

Vivian and Jake nodded at each other. They'd do what Price had, presumably, done in Uzbekistan, escaping overland rather than through an international airport.

"Even overland, Israel's going to be more tightly locked down than Uzbekistan," Jake said to Vivian, "but I like our chances a lot better that way than trying to fly out."

He turned to Dr. Peretz. "We're taking your minivan," Jake explained apologetically. "I'm sorry. It will be found later." The treasure hunter paused briefly before continuing, "I want you to hear it from me as well; we've done nothing illegal or untoward in Israel. Or anywhere else. You've been a wonderful host. You don't owe us anything but if your memory stayed a bit fuzzy for a few hours after the police get here, we'd really appreciate it." As an afterthought, he added "Someday, we'll buy you dinner and tell you what this is all about."

Minutes later, they were in the minivan. The Peretzs' apartment building shrank rapidly in the rearview mirror. As they turned onto the main road, three police cars and a tactical van passed them rushing the other direction, their lights blazing and sirens blaring. The convoy sped toward the Peretzs' building. Vivian didn't envy Michael and the boys for what they would come home to.

Chapter Twenty Five

Jake guided their vehicle onto a highway. As the passing distance markers indicated they traveled toward Jerusalem, Vivian spoke. "No offense, Jake, but I'm pretty sure the border between Israel and the West Bank isn't the border we want to try and finesse our way across."

Chuckling, Jake responded, "No argument there. If I were a betting man, and I am, I'd wager the authorities will realize that, too. The last place they'll look for us is on the road to Jerusalem. Hopefully, that will buy us a few hours and let us play a little shell game."

Every police car and checkpoint they passed elevated Vivian's anxiety. Once they entered the labyrinthine and chaotic old neighborhood of central Jerusalem, her nerves neared their breaking point. His protestations to the contrary, Jake appeared headed straight for the border between the city's east and west. Practically at the border, he turned off the main road. Methodically cruising narrow side streets, he was clearly looking for something.

Jake broke into a broad grin as the minivan entered a large square which served as an informal bus station. Crowds filled the square. Its four interlocking streets were jammed with buses, passenger vans, and taxis in every size, shape, and condition imaginable. People and vehicles so choked the roads that it made driving through nearly impossible. Slowly cruising the square, Jake found a parking space. "Okay," he said, "grab your stuff."

Exiting the minivan, her bag in hand, the thick clouds of diesel smoke gave Vivian a coughing fit. Jake wandered from bus to bus, briefly conversing with each driver in Arabic before moving along to the next vehicle. After a dozen such exchanges, his conversation with one driver lasted a little longer and ended with Jake handing him cash.

Vivian found herself on a rickety minibus carrying a crew of Palestinian construction workers to a jobsite in Eilat, a southern city which, conveniently for her and Jake, bordered both Egypt and Jordan. The construction workers were polite, almost deferential. But they could not conceal their curiosity, almost mystification, regarding the pair's presence among them. Vivian was certain the workers' friends and families would hear about the strange passengers that shared their bus ride. She also thought it unlikely such gossip would reach the ears of authorities. At least not in time to make a difference.

The bus reached Eilat the next morning, stopping in the smaller cousin of the Jerusalem square-turned-bus-station where their journey began. On foot, she and Jake made their way to the border crossing into Jordan. While Eilat also bordered Egypt's Sinai Peninsula, the pair hoped Israel's more congenial relations with Jordan might make border officials laxer. Additionally, once in Jordan, they could switch to a ferry at Aqaba. To use Jake's metaphor, that put one more shell in the shell game.

Vivian and Jake caught their first break in a while, reaching the border checkpoint just as a large group of American package tourists lined up to cross. Nonchalantly, they inserted themselves among the sunburned, conspicuously dressed travelers. It reminded Vivian of a quote. She couldn't remember the source but its gist was that the best place to hide a needle isn't a haystack. It was among other needles.

Though the passport control officers appeared to be moving the package tourists through with less than customary diligence, Vivian's unease returned. It reached fever pitch as two immigration guards methodically walked along the line of travelers waiting to cross. Submachine guns slung casually at their sides, they scrutinized each face in the line. Beside her, Jake tensed as well.

Taking her cue from a hundred bad spy movies, Vivian pulled Jake to her and kissed him, holding on tightly. As the guards reached the embracing pair, they halted. Vivian heard their whispers. When the guards broke into quiet laughter and continued down the line, she released the treasure hunter. The ruse worked. Still, Vivian scolded herself for not having to act more. Somewhere along the line, Jake Booker had learned to kiss.

As with the other tourists, the passport control officer stamped their passports and waved them through, barely glancing at their faces. They were now in the sleepy Red Sea resort town of Aqaba.

The ferry still hours away, Vivian and Jake drank tea at an outdoor café situated on a quiet street, surrounded by palm trees and ancient storefronts. Vivian couldn't relax. Not yet. The flipside to Jordan's stable relations with Israel was that Jordanian authorities might actively cooperate with them to locate two wanted antiquities smugglers. It didn't put her any more at ease when Jake excused himself, disappearing into a nearby curio shop. *We're international fugitives and he's buying souvenirs*, she thought, pouring another cup of tea.

"I've got something for you," Jake said, reappearing. Reaching into his pocket, he produced a small golden ring.

"Easy, cowboy," Vivian protested, "I don't know how they do things where you're from, but that kiss was just to throw off the guards."

"I know," Jake acknowledged, "and it was a great idea. The authorities are looking for two people, not one couple. Mental filters like that matter. What do you say? Think you could handle being hitched for a day or two?"

Vivian thought it over. It was not actually the worst proposal she'd had. Slipping the ring onto her finger, she joked "I do." Jake donned a matching men's ring.

Waiting for the ferry, they ordered a second pot of tea. Conversation turned to their travels. Perhaps unsurprisingly, Jake was more widely traveled. A true globetrotter, Vivian thought enviously. But, equally unsurprisingly, the countries that Vivian knew, she knew more deeply than Jake knew the myriad of spots he had visited.

Their discussion evolved to the topic of favorite archeological sites, the ones each found most impressive. She argued for Avebury, the massive stone circle, far larger than Stonehenge, in southwest England as well as the Great Pyramids. Jake advocated Angkor Wat, in Cambodia, and Petra, Jordan's massive "lost city" carved directly into rose-colored limestone cliffs.

It was one of those purely subjective topics where passions run high and that so easily turns into an argument. Before either of them knew it, they shouted over each other with voices raised to champion their respective sites. Realizing the absurdity of the argument, Vivian broke into laughter. "I'm sorry. Being married to me must be terrible."

"Not at all. Hell, you're way easier than the ex-Mrs. Booker."

Vivian raised an eyebrow. "So. There's an ex-Mrs. Booker?"

Jake nodded, his wide eyes proclaiming "You better believe it."

"What happened?"

"We grew apart. Actually, we started out further apart than either of us realized. I met her at a cotillion ball in college. She was very old money Dallas. You know, 5'5", but 6' 0" with the hair and heels," Jake laughed.

"There was nothing wrong with her," he continued. "She just wasn't right for me. When we were dating, she thought being married to an oil and gas man sounded interesting. After we got married, she realized it meant a lot of time apart and was really boring, to most people, anyway.

"One day, I got back from a long natural gas trip to Malaysia and found she'd taken up with a buddy of mine. That was the end of that. She's done really well for herself. She's a corporate VP now."

"Doesn't seem like you've done too badly for yourself either," Vivian observed.

"What about you, Doc? Ever married?"

Vivian shook her head. "No. Closest I've come was the guy I dated in undergrad. Freshman year all the way through to graduation. Poetry Major. I'll say this for him, he was gorgeous. Brilliant, too. I was impressed by his brilliance. He, I think, was impressed with mine. But there wasn't enough overlap. Byron and I ran out of things to talk about. I think a good relationship must involve not only finding someone who's smart, but someone who's the right kind of smart for you."

"Hold on a second," Jake said, "You dated a poetry major named Byron?"

Vivian blushed. She couldn't bring herself to add that, while also initially attracted to Byron's passion, it took her far too long to realize he channeled it all into his poetry. He could never quite bring it out in real life. After graduation, Byron had taken a knee, produced a ring and began, "At this stage in our lives, I think it makes sense that we…" He got no farther than that. Vivian, already having doubts, turned her back on the proposal. And the relationship. Compared with that, Jake Booker's "Hey, the authorities are looking for us," had been the pinnacle of romance.

The ferry's imminent departure brought an end to the conversation, allowing Vivian to avoid further disclosures.

In contrast with getting out of Israel, boarding a ferry for Egypt was a breeze. A finger of the Red Sea, the Gulf of Aqaba shared its parent's picturesque turquois color and abundant sea life. At one point, a pod of dolphins played in the ferry's bow wave. The rugged and picturesque desolation of the surrounding coastline rendered the water's fertility all the more vivid.

The pair had no trouble pulling off their marriage act convincingly. A few hours later, they arrived in Egypt.

Chapter Twenty Six

Sharm El Sheikh should not exist, Vivian reflected. From the panoramic window of their suite, she watched dusk descend upon the once sleepy Bedouin fishing village that had exploded into an international destination. On the streets below, Hollywood jetsetters, European fashionistas, Russian nouveau riche, and playboys from Dubai met and mingled. They basked on "Sharm's" broad sandy beaches, dived its warm waters, enjoyed the trendy nightlife, and shopped in its fashionable boutiques.

Jake was on good terms with the manager of one of Sharm's luxury hotels, who agreed to put them up for a few days, no questions asked. Turning from the window, she saw a grim expression on the treasure hunter's face. "We're safe here. For a long time, at least. But what's our next play?"

Sitting down on her bed, Vivian's pent-up rage and frustration burst forth. "This bastard has been one step ahead of us the entire way. He's got the Treasure Tablet. He's got whatever information was in the cave. He's got the materials he lifted from Herbert Price's collection. Plus anything that stayed in the family and never made it to Oxford. What have we got? Some weak leads scattered across the globe that might contain something useful. If we can find them. Jake, there's no way we're going to win this."

Jake remained silent as she spoke. When Vivian finished, he sat beside her.

"Look, I'm not good at compliments, but you may be the smartest person I've met. There's more than one solution to any problem. Somewhere out there is information that's going to lead us to Merlin's tomb." He chuckled. "Merlin's tomb. I can't believe I'm actually saying that. Your job is to find that information. You're going to sit down and Sherlock Holmes this thing."

"What are you going to do?"

"I'm going to think of a way to give Adrian Price a headache or two of his own."

"We should be able to turn up the legal heat on him," Vivian suggested. "After all, unlike us, he actually has stolen and smuggled antiquities."

"I'll get in touch with Abdulin and Grassley as well as the Oxford people to ensure they're all making a stink with the proper authorities about Price's activities. But, for three reasons, I think we need something else. First, from what you've said, the smart money is on the tomb being somewhere within the European Union. Unless he's left the EU since Oxford, he won't face passport or customs checks. Like in Uzbekistan, I doubt he was foolish enough to do his own dirty work in Israel, so I can't think of a reason he would leave. Second, he's had time to plan things. Even if we put some pressure on him, I expect he has contingencies in place. Third, it's pretty clear that he's not flustered by operating outside of the law."

Getting to work, Jake leaned over his tablet, occasionally glancing at copies of Herbert Price's materials they had made at Oxford. His normally playful features were replaced by an expression better suited to a bloodhound or wolverine.

Focusing on her laptop, Vivian reflected on everything the two of them learned about Myrddin and everything known or speculated over the centuries.

On her notepad, Vivian listed Myrddin's reputed final resting places. The stele and Treasure Tablet both indicated he intended to be buried in the place of his birth. Almost every source stated Myrddin was either Welsh or Breton. She hoped they were right. Bringing up online maps of Wales and France's Brittany Peninsula, she compared the alleged resting places with ancient and modern place-names. Finding something that remained overlooked for centuries was a longshot, but it offered a place to start.

Broceliande Forest was an early favorite. People, even scholars, frequently identified it with the modern forest of Paimpont in Western France. The two names were distant cognates. Better yet, Paimpont contained an alleged tomb of Merlin. A photo of that structure did not inspire confidence. The haphazard pile of small rocks looked more like someone's idea of a Celtic tomb than the real thing. It also seemed an unlikely monument to a man who had walked half the earth.

Vivian considered another possibility. Maybe "Broceliande" didn't refer to the forest. In the Common Brittonic of the sixth century, the word could be interpreted as "Region of the Horses." Perhaps that referred to the presence of horses, horse breeders, or a temple to Epona, the Celtic Goddess of Horses? That seemed plausible, but described so many places that only extensive research would narrow it down.

Bel Nemeton, another commonly reputed resting place, meant "Sacred Grove of Bel," the Celtic Sun God. Not a promising match for contemporary geography. But sacred groves offered an angle worth pursuing. Vivian brought up a list of known or suspected groves, paying special attention to one in Britany's Nevet Woods.

A quick search, however, revealed a problem with the Nevet Woods grove. Sometime during the sixth century, St. Ronan established a hermitage there. It seemed unlikely the saint would allow Myrddin, whose paganism was well attested to by the Sogdian manuscripts in Berlin as well as by Herbert Price's collection, to build his tomb there. Still, it remained implausible, not impossible. Vivian kept the Nevet Forest grove in her back pocket in case nothing else panned out.

She turned to more obscure potential resting places. Results were not encouraging. Jake's laughter disrupted her thoughts.

"Oh, Adrian," the treasure hunter's voice echoed through the suite, addressing their rival as if he was there, "You've been sloppy. I didn't expect such a rookie mistake." Jake glowed as he turned to Vivian, "It seems our buddy Price has been plagiarizing his ancestor's work."

She joined Jake in laughter as he showed her ideas, sentences, and even whole paragraphs from the elder Price's materials that appeared verbatim within Adrian Price's publications. It was perfect, Vivian agreed. Everything she knew about their adversary argued that pricking his hubris by calling his brilliance and reputation into question would fluster the man in a way no legal entanglement ever could. Such flustering, she hoped, would led to rash decisions and careless mistakes.

First, they had to make the information public and ensure Price knew he had been outed. Vivian forwarded all the evidence of Price's plagiarism that Jake compiled to several friendly archeologists, both at her university and elsewhere. Calling in a few small favors, Vivian ensured that charges of plagiarism against Adrian Price would soon appear all over social media.

"Excellent work," Vivian complimented, "what are you going to do now?"

"I'm going to take a nap," he replied, "and you're going to get back to finding that tomb."

As he settled onto his bed, Vivian studied Jake. The artificial light cast by her laptop screen accented the treasure hunter's age. He must be nearing fifty, in contrast to her nearing forty.

Attempting to refocus on the computer, her attention wandered instead. Vivian gazed at her bracelet. She remained enchanted by its beauty and syncretic blend of Celtic and Roman designs. In her mind, an idea blossomed. Roman culture was well established in Gaul by the sixth century. Traces of it lingered in Britain as well. That led to many hybrids. Not only material hybrids, like the bracelet, but linguistic ones as well.

What if Myrddin's tomb became obscured by such a hybrid, the original name of its location corrupted or fully translated by the interplay between Brittonic and French or Brittonic and English over the intervening fourteen centuries?

Vivian returned to her prime suspects, Bel Nemeton and Broceliande. In English, the latter meant "region of horses" and in French "lieu de chevaux." Both of those she found only as descriptions, never as a specific place name. A literal translation of "Sacred Grove of Bel" seemed even less likely to survive into modern times, especially without being well

148

known to Celtophiles around the world.

Phonetically, Bel resembled "Val," French for valley. Because "Val" was a common component of place names, it made a promising candidate for linguistic corruption. The hybrid Val Nemeton, "Valley of Sacred Spaces," sounded both appropriate and plausible. A search revealed place names translating as "Sacred Valley" in Ireland, a bit far to be promising but maybe worth putting in the back pocket, as well as Nepal and Peru, not even worth considering.

Looking at other words from sixth century Celtic languages with the same root as *nemeton*, Val Nemeto would be the "Valley of Aloneness. Or Loneliness. Or Solitude." Again, she returned to her maps.

There it was. La Vallee Isole, "The Isolated Valley." It was sufficiently close to the meaning of Val Nemeto. The remote spot on the Breton coast looked like a big, black X. But Vivian wanted confirmation, preferably something not dependent on the vagaries of millennium-old linguistic shifts.

Hours later, Jake woke. "Okay, Sherlock, the look on your face must mean you found something."

"La Vallee Isole in Brittany." She explained the linguistic reasoning behind her conclusion.

"Anything else?"

"Uh-huh. I can't believe Myrddin, a very old man at the time, made the journey home from Sogdia by himself. Especially if he was carrying treasure. He must have had help. The region around La Vallee Isole has a legend about a group of dark-skinned men arriving from the east. Written accounts of the legend date back to Charlemagne's time. That's two centuries after what we're looking for. Hopefully, it just took that long to write down."

"That's good," Jake nodded.

"It gets better. The region has some unique surnames. The names are gibberish if you treat them as Celtic, Romance, or Germanic words. But they're phonetically similar to some Uzbek surnames that happen to have Sogdian origins." Vivian beamed. "We're going to France."

She paused, her face losing some of its glow. "But how do

a couple of fugitives get there?"

Jake thought long and hard. "Our least bad option is this," he began, "I can get us on a freighter through the Suez Canal. Cargo crews get less scrutiny than passenger traffic, so we could probably sneak into Italy or Spain. Once we're in Europe, getting to France should be fairly easy. Emphasis on 'should.'"

"Sounds like you don't like that idea much?"

"There's a lot of 'shoulds' and 'maybes' in that plan. And it's the best one I can come up with. We'll need to look over our shoulders every minute. Even if we don't get caught, that will slow us down about as badly as if we had."

"What do you recommend?"

"Let's throw the dice. Maybe we were wrong to try to dodge this thing in Israel. Let's call my lawyers in Brussels. We'll fly straight to France, meet with the authorities, and make them put up or shut up. They shouldn't have a leg to stand on to detain us. If we show up acting indignantly rather than looking guilty by trying to dodge the authorities, it argues in our favor. And I think our odds are better making that one big bet than all the little bets we make by sneaking around."

It made sense. Vivian wished it didn't. But it did.

Chapter Twenty Seven

Constantinople stood far behind him as home drew ever nearer. Myrddin sheltered within the ancient trees as heavy rain fell in the open space beyond. Weather around the jagged mountains at Europa's heart was unpredictable. Normally pleasant, but given to sudden storms of terrible ferocity. Even as they trembled in the wind, the great boughs of the trees kept enough rain away to allow him to make fire.

Huddling around its warmth, dining on apples he'd picked, Myrddin noted the trees surrounding him. Here a yew. There an oak. Next to it, an ash. Further on, he saw alder, elder, and hazel. It pleased him that he'd found shelter in a natural sacred grove. Or was it? Myrddin's mind visualized the positions of trees back through many generations of natural seeding, arriving at an arrangement that would not be out of place in the sacred places of Britain. Druids had planted this grove. A very long time ago.

Curiosity stoked, Myrddin explored the woods. At its heart, he discovered a barrow. Stones placed at regular intervals covered the manmade mound. Almost certainly a grave. Examining the barrow, he located a deep divot in the hillside where soil long ago covered over its entrance.

No longer a young man, Myrddin's body had limits. But some things were worth today's exertion. And tomorrow's soreness. Slowly but steadily, Myrddin dug away at the earth blocking the tunnel into the barrow. When the hole grew large enough, Myrddin lit an oil lamp and descended the slick steps.

Flat stones lined the earthen wall. The crudely cut slates were incised with solar and lunar symbols, spirals, primitive scrollwork, stylized renderings of birds, and long fields of tally marks. As to the purpose of those tallies, Myrddin could only guess. An absence of grave goods argued the tomb had been plundered in the centuries, maybe even millennia, before erosion closed its entrance. That made it all the more remarkable that its occupant, and his personal possessions, remained unmolested.

Peering over the stone-lined crypt set into the floor, Myrddin stared into the eye sockets of his ancient antecedent. The skeleton's bony hands clutched a tall wooden staff. A golden torc encircled his neck. Majestic stag antlers were sewn to the remnants of his leather hood. It was said the druids of old wore such headgear. The man had been a Celt, or something very like a Celt. Could this be the first druid? Its improbability robbed the idea of none of its power.

Myrddin wished he could share the moment with someone who would appreciate it. Bleys? Bleys was dead. And if that was not quite the right word for it, it came close enough. Nimue might still live. But too much water stood between them, both literally and figuratively. The discovery was his alone to contemplate.

Always a collector, Myrddin yearned to take something to remember this moment by. But it seemed wrong to take from one whose tomb had already been pilfered. Even more, he feared taking from such a powerful individual, even a dead one. Especially a dead one, Myrddin corrected himself. In the end, he took only a small stone from that barrow's exterior. To balance the scales, Myrddin portioned out a part of his treasure and deposited it beside the ancient druid.

Afterward, by the fire, Myrddin reflected on the tomb's meaning. His people, he knew, once stretched across Gaul and Iberia. But so far east? How far had they once spread?

In his lifetime, he had witnessed Celtic domains in Gaul and Britain shrink to the benefit of others. Would Saxons, Romans, Franks, Goths, and others continue pushing Celts into ever smaller, more remote areas? What would happen if the land ran out? Where would they go?

In Alexandria, as the sages shared with him their idea of a spherical world, they explained one of their predecessors had gone further. Comparing the angle of shadows cast by the sun in various cities of Aegypt at the same time of day, the philosopher estimated the Earth's size. Save for the tiny islands off Eriu's western coast and the larger island chain said to be east of China, Myrddin had walked the known world's length. He had a rough idea of how far he traveled, and it covered but half of the ancient sage's estimate. Were the Alexandrians correct, vast oceans must stretch between Eriu and China. So vast that whole continents could be concealed therein.

That reflection triggered a faded memory. Myrddin recalled a very strange event in Eriu during a visit to that westerly island to consult sages there. At the time, he had missed its meaning but, now, he wondered if he once broke bread with tangible proof of those hidden continents.

Perhaps, with nowhere else to go, the Celts would one day go there. In lands yet unknown, they might build new cities and establish new kingdoms. The idea amused Myrddin as he drifted asleep.

Chapter Twenty Eight

Landing at Charles de Gaulle airport, Vivian and Jake were met by an escort. It was not, she reflected as the tough-looking gendarmes helped them into a police car, the kind of escort one wanted. Riding southwest through the French countryside toward nearby Paris, Vivian realized they had not been handcuffed. She wondered if that was a good omen.

She and Jake had discussed this at length. Yes, it was the best course of action. Yes, it gave them the maximum chance of a successful outcome. It still made her nervous as hell. As she often did when nervous or unhappy, Vivian found solace by losing herself in history.

Like so much of Europe, scratching Paris deeply enough revealed Celts. Long before the days of Caesar's campaign in Gaul, the City of Lights had been called Lutetia. Celts from the Parisii tribe founded the settlement. *No prizes for guessing where the city's current name comes from.* The Parisii had been part of larger confederation called the Suessiones. They spoke the Transalpine dialect of Gallic, one of the Continental Celtic languages. Today, that dialect, that language, and that entire language family, were as dead as the men who spoke it while rebelling against the Romans in 52 BC.

Vivian needed to rethink much of what she knew about history. Herbert Price speculated that Myrddin met with Charlemagne's Frankish ancestors at the beginning of his wanderings and passed through the lands of the Merovingian Kings upon his final return. Either encounter could have brought the sage through the streets of what, even then, stood as one of Europe's up and coming centers of culture and power.

Half an hour after departing the airport, their police car was waved through the elaborate iron gates of the Palais de Justice. The imposing erstwhile palace had served as the seat of French jurisprudence since the Middle Ages. Vivian grimaced ruefully as the vehicle parked in the Cour du Mai, the darkly storied courtyard in front of the palace. This courtyard gave the world the phrase "heads will roll." At the time, it hadn't been figurative.

Vivian hoped she and Jake would fare better. The gendarmes escorted them inside the palace to a marble-floored antechamber set up as a meeting room. It was already full. Upon entering, they were greeted by Jake's Brussels lawyers. The calm, professional, and immaculately-dressed men and women wore expressions that reminded Vivian of hatchets.

Unfortunately, the forces arrayed against them were at least as impressive. They included assistant deputy ministers from both the Ministry of Culture, because the matter involved archeology, and Ministry of Justice, because it involved alleged wrongdoing. Though both men radiated intelligence, the gaze of the second was as hard as the first's was soft. A representative from the European Commission gave the EU an informal presence at the meeting. The silver-haired woman's pleasant expression couldn't mask the aura of someone who preferred to be elsewhere. A vulpine-faced senior detective from Interpol rounded out the list.

After some heavily forced civility on all sides, the meeting began in earnest. The senior detective laid out the accusations against Vivian and Jake: smuggling, violating the Antiquities Act, and possible vandalism of a site possessing historical or archeological significance. He also pointed out that, though nothing ever went to trial, Jake Booker's reputation regarding antiquities was questionable at best. Now, the detective implied, the pair came to France to work who knew what mischief.

The French officials wanted Vivian and Jake detained until the matter could be sorted. The detective demanded detention and immediate extradition to Israel. The woman from the European Commission took a more conciliatory position, observing it seemed premature to discuss outcomes.

Insisting their clients stay silent, Jake's legal team fired back a salvo of its own. Accused by whom? On what evidence? Wasn't this just a witch hunt to cover up that the authorities couldn't find Price, the real criminal? Terms like "unlawful detention" and "hearsay" were tossed around frequently.

The lawyers had arranged for Drs. Grassley and Abdulin to be video-conferenced in from Uzbekistan to give informal testimony. Grassley seemed irked at the inconvenience and the preposterousness of the charges, but remained civil in recounting the theft of the Treasure Tablet and ongoing problems with theft at the dig site. Problems he now connected with Price. Attesting to his long relationship with Vivian and to her good character, the venerable excavator also pointedly recalled Vivian and Jake's attempt to safeguard the Treasure Tablet, at potential risk to life and limb.

He vanished from the monitor, giving way to his colleague. Unlike Dr. Grassley, Dr. Abdulin did not mince words in highlighting the absurdity of an international manhunt to detain Vivian and Jake while Adrian Price remained at large. The archeologist, in fact, displayed a knowledge of particular parts of the English language which would make a sailor blush.

Following the archeologists' video conference, animated conversation resumed in the meeting room. Among the forces of law and order, only the Interpol detective now seemed inclined to detain the pair, almost manically so. Vivian's mouth fell open when he asserted that she and Jake might actually be in cahoots with Price in stealing the Treasure Tablet. Or that they had arranged the tablet's theft themselves and killed Price to frame him.

On that last point, regardless of the lawyers' insistence he keep quiet, Jake could not resist adding, "Despite about a thousand witnesses who can place Price at Oxford and very much alive."

The detective was so much more vehement about detaining them than the other three were about letting them go free that Vivian feared the others might acquiesce simply to shut him up. With that chilling thought, Vivian made her move. Standing, in a voice one step shy of shouting, she interjected herself into the conversation.

"With us detained, Dr. Price will be free to loot the archeological find of the decade, if not the century, from under France's nose." Vivian did not spell out what she meant. She didn't need to. Everyone in the room had a dossier detailing events in Uzbekistan. They knew what information the Treasure Tablet purportedly contained. She was playing dirty, Vivian admitted to herself. Since the Second World War, the idea of having their art and antiquities pilfered invariably, and understandably, gave the French nightmares.

Playing dirty paid off. The next time the Interpol detective repeated his demands for detention and extradition, the Assistant Deputy Minister for Culture less than cordially invited him to butt out of France's internal affairs.

Departing the Palais de Justice, Vivian smiled. Her head remained attached to her shoulders. She and Jake had every prospect of remaining at liberty. The forces of law and order agreed no action would be taken against them until thorough investigations had been completed. And, of course, only if evidence of guilt emerged. She couldn't be certain about Interpol, but she suspected France and the EU wouldn't be investigating too hard. Indeed, she left the building with the Assistant Deputy Minister for Culture's business card and mobile phone number in her handbag, with instructions to call if he could be of any assistance.

Jake couldn't resist teasing her, "Seems like someone has a cabinet member sweet on her."

"Assistant deputy cabinet member, thank you very much. Besides, I don't think he's sweet on me. I think he's sweet on the treasure. Just like someone else I could mention."

Jake took the turnabout with aplomb before becoming serious, "There is something that bugs me about all this."

Vivian looked at him as if to say, *Only one thing?*

"Getting a couple of local polizei to freak out in Berlin is one thing. Making the Israelis go crazy and putting a hornet in Interpol's pants is something else entirely. And it wasn't just professional obligation, that detective was coming after us hard. It suggests a lot more weight that I'd have given Price credit for. Maybe I'm wrong. Maybe he's got the weight. Or is that good. Or just that lucky."

"You think he's got a bigger fish behind him?" Vivian asked. "But who?"

Jake didn't have an answer. Neither did Vivian. That didn't make her like the question.

Finally free from worry, on one matter at least, they boarded a train for Brittany. Vivian felt relief there had been no direct encounters with Price or his minions recently. So far. As their train rolled through the hills and woodlands of the Breton Peninsula, Vivian reviewed her notes. Jake was engrossed in his tablet.

"You won't believe this," he said.

"What?"

"So, according to the *Golden Bough,* not only does the village nearest to La Vallee Isole still preserve folk memories of visitors arriving from the east, the event is commemorated in their annual Solstice festival. Or, at least it was when Frazer was writing in 1890."

"You have a copy of the *Golden Bough* on your tablet?"

"Doesn't everyone?"

Vivian changed subjects. "I've found a potential complication."

"Which is?"

"Many tombs, from Neolithic to Iron Age, have been identified in the valley. How do we figure out which one is the right one?"

Jake looked thoughtful, "I don't think that will be a problem. Myrddin doesn't seem like a guy who would travel the world without learning a few new things. If I was a betting man, and I am, I'd wager that his tomb doesn't resemble anything else in the valley. Are there any pictures?"

"Not of every tomb in the valley, but some."

Sharing Vivian's laptop, they examined her images. They knew it the moment they saw it. The overhead image came from a 2007 aerial survey by the University of Rennes. Jake was right, it differed from every other structure in the area. Its

158

base was carved directly into the valley's rocky slope with tiers of concentric squares resting on top. Vivian knew no regular Breton, Gaul, or Roman built this. The survey indicated the structure remained unexcavated, or at least was unexcavated in 2007.

Their train pulled into Quimper, the ancient town at the heart of old Brittany. Church bells sounded over the half-timbered buildings of the old town. Discussing how best to proceed, Vivian and Jake walked the footbridges crisscrossing the confluence of the three rivers that were Quimper's lifeblood. Though they were more than five miles from the ocean, she swore the strong breeze carried the invigorating scent of the sea.

After some debate, the pair decided there was still merit in trying to blend in and keeping a low profile. Even if they no longer needed to stay below the authorities' radar, there remained value in avoiding Price's attention. Eager to be inconspicuous and leave no trail which could be easily followed, they caught an intercity bus to Bocages, the village nearest the valley.

The past week had strengthened Vivian's faith in the power of serendipity. She was only half-surprised to realize their arrival coincided with the Summer Solstice festival Jake discovered within the *Golden Bough's* pages.

Chapter Twenty Nine

Bocages was postcard perfect. Aside from its bus station, municipal building, schoolhouse, and a service station, no building appeared to date from after the Industrial Revolution. Many of its buildings were half-timbered relics, some of its cottages still thatched, looking as if they might predate the Revolution.

They checked into a pension on its cobblestoned main street. Too late in the day to head to the valley, Vivian and Jake rested in their room before joining the festival.

The festival procession began with a marching band, leading the rest of the parade with cacophonic brass and woodwind arrangements of traditional Breton folk music. They were followed by members of Bocages' civic organizations and an open-topped limousine carrying its mayor, the local National Assembly representative, and their spouses. Trailing behind the limousine was a phalanx of morisques, the French equivalent of mummers and Morris dancers, clad in outrageous costumes adorned with garlands and colorful ribbons.

After the morisques, four revelers donning oversized papier-mâché carnival masks paraded down the street. Their painted heads were the color of café au lait, with black hair, black eyes, and attired as per traditional European images of Moors. This was what they had read about in the *Golden Bough*. But it was the fifth figure, sandwiched between the quartet of Moors, which commanded Vivian's attention. His papier-mâché mask was fair-skinned, with snow white hair and black lines evocative of wrinkles. He wore a robe and a white beard dangled from the mask's chin down to the cobblestones. As the five figures walked, their outsized heads bobbing comically, they tossed sweets and coins to children in the crowd.

Following this quintet was another wave of morisques. At the end came the père of the village church. Swinging a silver censer that billowed pungent incense smoke, the priest was flanked by young acolytes. With this final note in the procession, it was as if the church, rather sheepishly, wanted to give a veneer of religious respectability to the festival's obvious pagan overtones.

After the procession passed, the festival became a street party. Wine, song, and food flowed freely. Vivian and Jake partook as freely as tomorrow's activities allowed. The treasure hunter's many talents, she noted, did not include a fine singing voice. Rambunctious children ran through the chaos, tossing eggs, flour, and the occasional firecracker. As the hour grew late and the outdoor festivities were increasingly claimed by reckless youth and amorous adolescents, the pair retired to the tavern adjacent to their pension.

At the bar, Vivian introduced herself to the proprietress. Anne-Marie was a sturdy woman whose good health had clearly endured into late middle age. It pleased Vivian to learn that she bore one of the unique surnames discovered in her research. Physically, however, nothing distinguished her from other villagers she had seen. Anne-Marie seemed charmed by Vivian's not quite fluent Breton and enjoyed the opportunity to practice her own English. As the wine glasses emptied, both women found themselves switching haphazardly from one language to the other. Quickly scanning the tavern, she spotted Jake sitting in the corner, chatting animatedly with men from the village who puffed on old-fashioned pipes as they talked.

Eventually, Vivian asked the question she wanted to hear Anne-Marie answer. "So, what's with the figures with the big papier-mâché heads?"

"Well, my grandmere, she always insisted it was something that actually happened here in Bocages many centuries ago. But now, most people don't think that. They say it represents the Magi coming to adore the Christ Child, or the legend of Prester John, or some bit of lost pagan ritual."

Interesting explanations all, Vivian thought. Of course, if the procession represented the Magi, why hold it during the Summer Solstice? Whether coincidence or garbled folk

161

memory, the Prester John story held a kernel of truth. Sogdia, like the mythical Prester John's kingdom, had been filled with Nestorians. Vivian suspected Myrddin would be horrified that his arrival became linked with the monotheistic Nestorians.

Before retiring to her room, Vivian asked Anne-Marie if there were any taxis or cars for rent in the village. The older women informed her that several young men in Bocages could be hired as drivers, preferring such odd jobs to the tedium of steady work. On a napkin, she wrote down a couple of names and numbers for Vivian.

The next morning, Vivian made some calls. She secured the services of two surly twenty-somethings and their beat-up Citroën. The car, she realized, was older than the young men in the front seat.

Leaving tiny, picturesque Bocages behind, they drove into the Breton countryside. Though they headed toward the sea, a line of hills loomed ahead. While the hills could not be very high, their steep slope and jagged profile rendered them menacing. On the other side, Vivian realized, was La Vallee Isole.

One way or another, their quest would end there. And it had been a quest, in the fullest sense of the word. Though the world might never know of it, Vivian shivered at the realization she and Jake had written themselves into the story of Arthur, of Camelot, and, above all, of Merlin.

The Citroën turned from the main road onto a tiny path between two hedgerows, shattering her reverie. Vivian frowned. Perhaps this backroad took them closer to the valley. Still, it didn't feel right. They traveled parallel with the line of hills rather than toward it. After a quarter mile, the car came to a stop. In the front seat, one young man produced a tire iron as the other drew a butcher knife.

"You're kidding me! Not again." She cursed.

Jake addressed the boys in rapid French. They did not stop.

"You told them whatever he's paying, you'd double it?" Vivian asked.

"Not exactly."

She arched an eyebrow.

"Like someone suggested, I told them, 'Whatever he or she is paying you, I'll double it.'"

"They don't look impressed," Vivian commented and gave it a try. Unlike Jake's French, her Breton got results. The young men froze, seemly reconsidering their actions. Playing a hunch, she pressed the issue. In her experience, in small communities around the world, the threat of social sanction was a powerful motivator. Often more powerful than legal sanction. "Anne-Marie gave me your names and numbers," Vivian said, invoking the colorful matriarch, "She'll be very disappointed if she finds out what you're doing."

An outlay of cash from Jake sealed the deal. As it turned out, with a little extra pressure from her, Jake's "I'll double it" attitude worked once again. As the boys turned-coat and spilled their guts, Vivian translated for Jake.

"Price has most of Bocages' ne'er-do-wells on his payroll," she summarized. "This pair says there are two walkable passes through the hills into La Vallee Isole. Price is having both of them watched. Otherwise, it takes an actual climb to get into the valley. Without fighting our way in, I don't know how we're going to get over the hills."

"We're not going over them. We're going to go under them."

Jake grinned as she looked at him quizzically.

"My original training is in geology, remember? Petroleum geology, granted, but geology nonetheless. These hills are part of a formation called the Armorican Massif, a band of sedimentary rock stretching from here to central France. Last night, it struck me that these hills must be shot through with caves."

"You found one?"

"Yeah. While you were talking to the bartender, I talked with some guys from the village. There's a cave called the Sentier d'Ermites, the Trail of Hermits, running all the way into the valley."

"Wonderful. How do we get there?"

"If we can get your new hooligan pals to give us a lift, we

163

can hike there from the roadway in half an hour or so." Jake tossed her his canvass bag. "I brought some water and two heavy-duty flashlights."

Back on the main road and another mile toward the sea, the young men let Vivian and Jake out at a place where the blacktop crossed a small stream. Along the waters, an overgrown and seldom-used footpath wound its way toward the hills.

As they walked, Jake shared what he learned about the cave's rich history. It had been used as a base by the Resistance during World War Two. Local tradition also claimed a group of Templars took refuge there after the disbanding of their order in the thirteenth century. Older folklore linked the cave with pre-Christian mystery cults. And it played host to Paleolithic cave paintings, like those at Lascaux a couple hundred miles away.

Vivian had pictured something larger. The tiny fissure Jake indicated was only a couple feet taller and wider than a person. At least they were alone. Price either didn't know about the cave or didn't expect them to know. Unless guards lurked inside the cave or at the far end, she thought unpleasantly.

"Done much spelunking?" Jake inquired.

"Nope."

"Let me go first on this one."

Vivian marveled at the complete darkness. Even their powerful flashlights succeeded only in cutting slices out of the omnipresent black. She imagined the experience from the perspective of someone carrying only an oil lamp, torch, or nothing it all. Small wonder caves once featured so prominently in humanity's rites and rituals.

Not far inside, they found the cave paintings. Evocative profiles of deer, wild horses, birds, and fish were rendered in pigments of black, brown, red, and white. Like the painters themselves, some of the animals pictured, aurochs, cave hyenas, and European bison, now inhabited only the past.

Further in, paintings gave way to petroglyphs. Mother goddess imagery, warrior figures, concentric circles, and spirals were incised into the rock with great care. Vivian's training was insufficient to tell if they were Celtic in origin, dated from earlier in the Bronze Age, or were a mix of both. She would definitely tell the archeology department about this place. Assuming she survived the next few hours.

Ducking dangling stalactites and sidestepping the looming stalagmites required constant attention. "You can always remember which is which," she fleetingly recalled her Seventh Grade science teacher saying, "because stalac*tites* must hold tight to avoid falling."

Darkness consumed her sense of time. It felt as if they had been walking forever. This, too, yielded insight into the awe with which earlier peoples regarded caves. When Vivian finally spotted a pinprick of light ahead, she did feel a little like Persephone returning to the sunlit lands.

Chapter Thirty

He felt badly for the young men who accompanied him on his journey. True, they thought it an honor. But it was unlikely they would see their homes and families again. Of course, several of them had already found girls from the farming village. Myrddin was happy for them.

He was more ambivalent that some of them had also found the God of Rome. But perhaps not as ambivalent as he once would have been. He could not deny that, on his return journey, the pious Princess Radegund had impressed him.

Of course, that encounter was also tied up with feelings about his reunion with L'Ancel. It amused Myrddin that the man now answered to the name which once enraged him. Their meeting had been, if not good, at least cathartic. It had only been Arthur's pride, Myrddin now admitted to himself, which prevented the king from summoning L'Ancel before Camlann. Despite everything that had transpired, or perhaps because of it, if Arthur had called, the man and his retainers would have come. But now, in his winter years, the once fierce warrior had taken holy orders.

Like Myrddin and L'Ancel, the old ways were dying.

Myrddin's tomb would be less than a bowshot from the village where he was born. The stone huts, once filled with the laughter and songs of fishers and weavers, stood empty now. By appearances, they had been abandoned many years. Myrddin wondered what became of his people. The newcomers from the farming village beyond the valley could not tell him.

Sometimes, at dawn and dusk, Myrddin saw the ghosts of his people. They could not see or hear him. At least they gave no indication of such. But, with each passing day, their shades grew more distinct.

He had visited the tiny hut that had witnessed his entry into the world. He recalled his mother cradling him, singing to him for the first time, as the midwives cut the umbilical cord. Myrddin remembered his own birth. As Bleys and Nimue remembered theirs. He could not be certain, but would not be surprised if that also held true for the elderly wu at the Sui Emperor's court and crazed King Shaddad of Irem. It was part of what set their kind apart from normal people. He and Bleys argued many times over what it meant. His mentor felt it was the cause of their intrinsic difference. Myrddin suspected it offered an omen or hallmark of what made them different, not the cause itself. Had there always been such individuals? Perhaps the Alexandrian sage who had given measure to the earth itself and the ancient druid interred in the shadows of Europa's great mountains were as well. And would there always continue to be?

Myrddin sat on the same turtle-shaped rock that fascinated him as a boy. So many days he had played on and around it. Even among his people, Myrddin was a strange child. Sometimes he had talked to the rock—whispered secrets to it. It never failed to appreciate his insights or keep his confidences. Now, he rested on it as he watched the construction of his tomb. He wondered if some of his magic had found its way into the rock.

The men from the new village beyond the valley were good natured but often regarded him strangely as they worked on his tomb. Certainly, they had never seen one like it. He wondered if the world had ever witnessed such a structure. In his travels, Myrddin had encountered amazing things, wondrous things. Perhaps even miraculous things. Many of those he would conceal inside. Those too big to carry with him, he paid tribute to on its outside. What the men from the new village thought was not his problem. His final problem was figuring out how to safeguard his treasure. As he considered the matter, Myrddin began to mix the pigments.

Chapter Thirty One

La Vallee Isole was a place apart. Geography and climate conspired to create a world utterly unlike the one on the other side of the hills. Initially, Vivian noticed the wind. The narrow valley, more accurately a box canyon opening onto the ocean, funneled the sea breezes into formidable gusts. She tucked her dark hair under her ball cap.

The blues of sea and sky seemed deeper and more vivid than normal. Sunshine so potent it was almost tangible bathed the valley, as if she was somehow closer to the sun. Compared with the riotous fertility of the rest of Brittany, vegetation here was sparse. Stunted by the salty air and twisted by the wind, diminutive pines, little taller than Vivian, reminded her of bonsai trees. Clumps of resilient shrubs and hearty coastal grasses clung to their precarious existence in the windswept valley.

Patches of bare rock poked through the thin soil. Stones, from pebbles to boulders, were strewn throughout the valley. Some clustered tightly together, forming shapes and outlines the eye eventually recognized as the work of human hands.

From its stony beach, the valley floor rose sharply to the canyon's far end. Vivian and Jake started up the slope to where a wide ledge doubled-back towards the ocean, ending in a promontory that jutted hundreds of feet over the waves. According to GPS coordinates from the University of Rennes survey, the structure she identified as Myrddin's tomb sat near the end of that ledge, overlooking the ocean.

As they walked, Vivian was flooded by a mixture of excitement, reverence, and trepidation. In the distance, one of the strangest structures either of them had encountered came into view. Nearly at the precipice of the ledge, its ground level was carved directly into the Armorican limestone. Several faux-stories built from local stones rested on top, each diminishing in width and length from the one below.

"It looks like a damn ziggurat," Jake said, mirroring her thoughts. The ground level, however, reminded her of

Ethiopia's carved churches.

"Yes, yes, it's a very curious structure."

Vivian's blood ran cold, realizing it hadn't been Jake that spoke.

Turning around, she found Adrian Price stalking them from behind. He clenched a pistol firmly in one hand.

"Apparently, I am a slow learner," he said. "After Samarkand, I should have figured out the only way to take care of the two of you is to do it myself."

"Price, I still don't get it," Vivian said. "If you had played it straight, you would still get most of the glory from this. Why do you want to keep it to yourself so badly?"

"There's the principle of it all. By right of our descent from Herbert Price, this site is my family's to do with as we wish. My ancestor also had some curious notions about what the tomb might contain and about what 'Merlin's Treasure' really meant. Just in case he was right, I need to examine it before anyone else."

"What kind of notions?"

Instead of answering, Price pointed the barrel of the gun towards the edge of the promontory. "We are going to take a walk now."

When Vivian and Jake were ten feet ahead, too far to rush him, Price followed. As she walked, Vivian berated herself for having found the man attractive on their first meeting. Price, meanwhile, launched into the kind of monologue she assumed occurred only in movies.

"After washing my hands of the two of you in Samarkand, I smuggled myself out of Uzbekistan into Kazakhstan across what remains of the Aral Sea in the hull of a rusting Soviet fishing boat. You're no doubt wondering about the fate of the Treasure Tablet, so I'll save you the suspense. I memorized it before leaving the country. Then I smashed it and scattered the pieces in sea."

Jake scowled and Vivian moaned softy in horror. Compared to defacing Joseph of Arimathea's Cave and multiple thefts from Oxford, to say nothing of attempting to murder her and Jake, the Treasure Tablet was a small thing.

But Vivian's scholarly heart cringed anytime a unique source of information disappeared from the world.

Price delighted in her outrage, "Of all the pleasures life offers, my dear Dr. Cuinnsey," he commented, "None is sweeter than being the only person in the world who knows something important. You should try it sometime."

"In Kazakhstan, I enjoyed a first class flight from Almaty to Moscow. About that time, my contacts reported that the two of you were still alive and departing Uzbekistan. I realized, if I was in your shoes, knowing next to nothing, the Ethnological Museum of Berlin presented the obvious destination. And poor Dr. Grassley and Dr. Abdulin are nothing if not obvious.

"During your interrogation in Berlin, I had a nice, relaxed crossing into Eastern Europe and, from there, to France. By that time, I already worked out that Myrddin's tomb was in Brittany.

"I confess, Mr. Booker threw a big spanner in my plans. It wasn't until later that I learned he and I shared an alma mater. With the possibility he might be familiar with my great-grandfather's work, or simply stumble across it while searching the Bodleian, I had to put everything on hold and try to secret away my family's remaining materials before you got to them. And, as you know, that reckless chase the two of you insisted upon at Oxford very nearly cost me the game."

"I believe that was the whole point," Vivian smirked.

Price ignored her jibe. "Fortunately, I had known Joseph of Arimathea's Cave was a liability. Such information was too valuable to be left someplace where just anyone could stumble across it. Don't feel bad there. I had that taken care of quite a while ago. So, regardless of the other difficulties you tried to put in my path, I could return to Brittany and focus on deciphering the Treasure Tablet's riddle. You will, however, both pay for calling my reputation as a scholar into question."

At that last sentiment, Jake gave a quiet but very satisfied chuckle.

As they marched, Vivian stepped in scree. As the loose stones scattered beneath her, she lost her footing. From the ground, she saw Jake regarding her with concern as Price watched with irritation. Standing, she hissed as she put weight on the foot.

"Sprained," she said between clenched teeth.

"In a few moments it won't matter anyway." With the muzzle of his gun, Price motioned for Jake to assist her. One arm wrapped firmly around her, Jake helped Vivian hobble along. Every few steps she gasped from putting too much weight on the ankle.

"So, Price," Vivian asked, "What did the Treasure Tablet say?"

Adrian Price repeated the Common Brittonic inscription on the tablet. Giving careful attention to the inscription's rhyme and meter, and recited in his Welsh-tinted Oxbridge accent, Vivian thought it sounded magnificent. Her nemesis certainly possessed a theatrical flourish. When Price finished, she translated for Jake.

> *Mirdin, Great Counselor, departs*
> *To die. To rest. In the place of his people*
> *To the wilds and waters of the Little Big Land*
> *Hunting the Fixed Star*
> *From the Child of Three Mothers*
> *To the Sea-Song Prison*
> *And, from there, overlooks all.*

"The first two lines were just context," Price said, "'Wilds and waters of the Little Big Land' provided the first real clue. Like Great-Grandfather Herbert, and all my forefathers, I hoped Myrddin was Welsh. But, unlike Herbert, not so passionately that I couldn't see other possibilities. Had my ancestor not been so insistent on that particular point, I suspect he might have discovered Myrddin's tomb a century ago.

"I realized that 'Little Big Land,' from the perspective of a sixth century Celt, very neatly described Brittany. The little Breton Peninsula attached to the much larger Europe. It was, at once, a land both bigger and smaller than the British Isles.

171

"With Brittany being 'Little Big Land,' then the 'child of three mothers' is Quimper, of course." Vivian added, having just the day before reflected upon the role of its three rivers in nurturing the city. Though she could not see Price's face, his pregnant silence said much. She concluded he had not worked that out nearly so easily or quickly as she had.

Price continued, "As far as 'hunting the fixed star...'"

"North" she and Jake said in unison, increasing Price's irritation. The phrase clearly referenced Polaris, more commonly called the North Star, which hung nearly immobile in the night sky. In conjunction with the previous clue, it gave instructions to travel north from Quimper.

"The hardest part of the riddle was 'the sea song prison,'" Price admitted. "I spent days pouring over topographic maps and place names before realizing it referred to a box canyon opening onto the sea. A place where canyon walls trap the sounds of the ocean. The only place north of Quimper fitting that description is La Vallee Isole."

Given the herculean mental effort Vivian required to identify La Vallee Isole, she could not fault Price for his difficulty there. Still, she thought smugly, she had done it without help from Myrddin's verbal map.

She noted that the recollections of Dr. Grassley and Dr. Abdulin regarding the Treasure Tablet's inscription, while fragmentary, had been essentially correct. The three mothers, the star, the sea, and the song. It had all been there. Vivian hoped she would live long enough to tell them.

"After ensuring I had an adequate base of operations in the area and, I thought, sufficient muscle in case the pair of you showed up, I came to the valley," he continued. "I was trekking to its highest point, which, as the Treasure Tablet concludes, 'overlooks all,' when I saw you two emerge into the sunlight from that blasted cave. So, concealing myself behind that boulder, I waited until you had passed."

The three made their way along the narrowing ledge to the lip of the promontory. Though beyond she could see only sky, Vivian's ears were dimly aware of the beckoning crash of waves far below.

"Unlike Uzbekistan," Price commented, "here I'm wary about leaving evidence. So, I'll let nature do the work for me. You'll both take a walk over that cliff. Even if they find your bodies, and that's a big 'if,' it's simply two more unfortunate accidents in the wilds of Brittany.

"I admit, you two have almost been worthy adversaries. Part of me regrets ridding myself of you. The smaller part, obviously."

"Price?"

"Yes, Mr. Booker?" The archeologist looked amused. "I assume this is your last, desperate plea?"

"Nope. I just wanted you to know you're a son of a bitch."

Price appeared taken aback by Jake's plainspoken trash-talk in the face of impending doom. As he was distracted, Vivian sprang atop a perfectly convex stone. Planting one foot against the solid rock, she kicked out with the other. As she connected firmly with Price's chest, the archeologist wheeled backward over the promontory's edge. Falling toward the waves, gun popping harmlessly into empty space, the wide-eyed surprise on his face was almost comic.

Then Price was gone.

"What the hell was that?" Jake laughed, "I thought your ankle was busted!"

"Someone once told me that it can pay to be underestimated. I decided to test that advice."

"What do you think?"

"I'll have to thank him sometime."

They embraced, relieved to be alive. Taking a deep breath, their attention turned to the megalithic structure behind them.

Chapter Thirty Two

Even as darkness gathered, Myrddin knew the sky was clear and it could not be long past noon. It was his light that dimmed, not the sun's. The tomb was complete and his treasure safeguarded within. He was confident only those worthy of such riches would find them.

As he rested comfortably on his pallet, the world went black. From a distance, the songs of wind and wave still reached his ears. Myrddin wondered what would come next. Would he dream? Would he find Arthur? Tarkun? Bleys? Nimue?

Chapter Thirty Three

A stone slab four feet tall and two feet wide blocked the tomb's single entrance. Fourteen hundred years of sediment covered its bottom. Improvising tools, Vivian and Jake dug away the sediment before turning attention to the monolith blocking the entrance. Using a pair of stout pine branches as levers, together they eventually moved the slab enough to wiggle inside.

The tomb's interior consisted of a single chamber, about thirty feet to a side, with a high ceiling. Plaster covered the walls, another distinctly un-Celtic touch. Or the remnants of plaster, anyway. Brittany was not Uzbekistan. The preservation climate here left only faint traces of once brilliant frescos. But enough survived for Vivian to see obvious similarities with those near Samarkand.

At the center stood a sarcophagus built from local stones and covered by a monolith much larger than the one that had blocked the entrance. This other stone would not be moved so easily. Perhaps that was just as well, Vivian thought. For now, at least, it seemed disrespectful to open the final resting place of a man as close to the Merlin of legend as to make no real difference.

In true Celtic fashion, the tomb swelled with grave goods. There were piles of bracelets, amulets, torcs, and similar creations. While mostly wrought of bronze or iron, Vivian saw some of silver and gold. Many contained inlays of tortoiseshell, abalone, and semi-precious stones. There were smaller piles of more valuable stones like amber and topaz as well as one of what appeared to be coffee beans, which had spilled over and covered most of a Go board. Next to the sarcophagus sat a fancy saddle of distinctly Central Asian appearance. A small statue of a Fu Dog rested against one of Anubis. A kite frame hid behind the statues, shreds of faded silk still clinging to the wood. And was that really a shofar in one corner?

More enigmatically, dozens of clay jars filled the tomb.

The vessels were sealed with resin that long ago became hard as concrete. They resembled Greek amphorae. Perhaps they contained grain, oil, and wine for Myrddin to use in the afterlife? They could also be canopic jars. But that raised very unpleasant questions about who all those organs would have belonged to.

In the end, when Jake suggested it was impossible to make an omelet without breaking eggs, professional ideals aside, she offered only token protest. The cowboy broke the top off a jar, revealing half a dozen tightly rolled sheets of vellum within. Long centuries had rendered them brittle. Carefully, Jake handed one to Vivian. "Okay, Doc, if it breaks, it's on your head not mine."

"Gee, thanks."

Gingerly, she unrolled the parchment. The pigment ink had faded over the centuries but Vivian could still discern the writing. Seemingly random sequences of characters filled the entire sheet. Arabic numerals, written in archaic styles, were interspersed with letters from the Latin alphabet and characters from Sogdian and other scripts.

"Some kind of encryption?" Jake wondered.

Vivian nodded, "has to be."

"What do you think they are?" he asked.

"No way to know until they're decrypted," she replied. "Myrddin's life story? His wisdom? Magic scrolls? All three? Whatever they are, this is the real treasure."

Epilogue

On the flight back to America, Vivian dozed. She was pleased with how things were turning out. The French government had been very cooperative about their discovery, thanks in no small part to her new friend, the Assistant Deputy Minister for Culture. They agreed to a ten year moratorium on announcing the site's location, to protect the integrity of the site and its contents as well as to give some advantage to those who risked life and limb discovering it. Vivian's university, along with a French institution to be named later, would share first rights to excavation and analysis.

Just translating and interpreting Myrddin's manuscripts could easily take ten years. His cypher, however, was falling faster than expected. In at least one way, the modern world had outfoxed the cunning old sage. Myrddin assumed anyone trying to crack his cypher would be unfamiliar with decimal-based mathematics; that it would be secret knowledge rather than part of daily life for billions of people.

Police had searched Adrian Price's London flat, his house in Swansea, and even some of the hidden passageways exposed by their chase beneath Oxford. Sadly, many of the materials already pilfered from Herbert Price's collection remained unaccounted for. A frustration, but, admittedly, small in comparison with her success…and her survival. The suggestion Jake voiced back in Paris, that a larger nemesis might stand behind Adrian Price, still troubled her. She tried not to think about it.

Jake's company would have the rights to a traveling museum exhibit about the tomb and its discovery, putting select pieces on display. It was already booked solid for the next decade, being hosted by the world's greatest museums: the British National Museum, Egyptian Museum, Hermitage, Louvre, National Museum of China, Neues Museum, Smithsonian, and the Vatican Museum, among others.

His company also had rights to produce a high profile documentary. If a few million people might visit the traveling exhibition, hundreds of millions would see the documentary. Oh yes, Jake Booker would get his fortune, just as he'd known he would. It would be a small fortune but a fortune nonetheless.

And he might end up with more than just a fortune, Vivian reflected. Whatever was between the two of them remained undefined for now. Undefined but delightful.

In a few hours, she would be curled up with Dart. The thought made her very happy. Next morning, she'd go into her office. The mountain of paperwork awaiting her did not make her happy. In fact, it almost made her wish she had jumped off that cliff in Brittany. Almost. After checking in at her office, Vivian would walk over to the archeology department and turn over the bracelet Dr. Grassley had given her. She smiled, observing its graceful form on her wrist.

Then again…

Additional Resources

The resources listed below provide a scholarly examination of many topics treated in this book. Because new information constantly comes to light and data is often open to interpretation, I cannot not vouch for all the information and interpretations these works offer, but all are useful sources for readers desiring a deeper look into these subjects. While most of the resources target a general audience, a few are heavily academic (a couple are, in fact, textbooks). Likewise, while many are available as eBooks or otherwise easily and inexpensively available, a handful are obscure and not easy on the wallet.

Britain, Post-Roman and Late-Roman
Campbell, James et all. *The Anglo-Saxons* (Penguin Books, 1991).
Cunliffe, Barry. *Britain Begins* (Oxford University Press, 2012).
Cunliffe, Barry. *Iron Age Britain* (Batsford Ltd., 2004).
De la Bedoyere, Guy. *Roman Britain: A New History* (Thames & Hudson, 2014).
Fleming, Robin. *Britain After Rome: The Fall and Rise, 400 to 1070.* (Penguin UK, 2012).
Snyder, Christopher A. *An Age of Tyrants: Britain and the Britons*, A.D. 400-600 (Penn State University Press, 1998).

Brittany
Galliou, Patrick et all. *The Bretons* (Wiley-Blackwell, 1996).
Piette, Gwenno. *Brittany: A Concise History* (University of Wales Press, 2008).

Celts
Cunliffe, Barry. *The Celts: A Very Short Introduction* (Oxford University Press, 2003).

"The Celts," *In Our Time*, BBC Radio Four, 2002, http://www.bbc.co.uk/programmes/p0054894

Haywood, John. *Atlas of the Celtic World* (Thames & Hudson, 2001).

James, Simon. *The World of the Celts* (Thames & Hudson, 2005).

Russell, Paul. *An Introduction to the Celtic Languages* (Routledge, 1995).

Linguistics, General

Burton, Strang et al. *Linguistics for Dummies* (For Dummies Publications, 2012).

Parker, Frank et al. *Linguistics for Non-Linguists* (Pearson, 2009).

Preston, John. "How to Decipher a 4,000-Year-Old Tax Return," *The Telegraph,* February 8, 2014. http://www.telegraph.co.uk/culture/books/10620324/How-to-decipher-a-4000-year-old-tax-return.html

Oxford University and the Bodleian Library

Brockliss, L.W.B. *The University of Oxford: A History* (Oxford University Press, 2016).

Clapinson, Mary. *A Brief History of the Bodleian Library* (Bodleian Library, University of Oxford 2015).

Evans, G.R. *University of Oxford: A New History* (I.B. Tauris, 2013).

Vaisey, David. *Bodleian Library Treasures* (Bodleian Library, University of Oxford. 2015).

Sogdia and the Silk Road

Baumer, Christoph. *The History of Central Asia: The Age of the Silk Roads* (I.B. Tauris, 2014).

Baumer, Christoph. *The History of Central Asia: The Age of the Steppe Warriors* (I. B. Tauris, 2012).

De las Vaissiere, Etienne, "Sogdians in China: A Short History and Some New Discoveries," http://www.silkroadfoundation.org/newsletter/december/new_discoveries.htm.

Hansen, Valerie. *The Silk Road: A New History* (Oxford University Press, 2015).

Marshak, Boris. "The Archeology of Sogdiana," http://www.silkroadfoundation.org/newsletter/december/archaeology.htm.

Marshak, Boris. *Legends, Tales, and Fables in the Art of Sogdiana* (Bibliotheca Persica, 2002).

Liu, Xinru. *The Silk Roads: A Brief History with Documents* (Bedford/St. Martin's, 2012).

Newitz, Annalee. "The Lost Empire that Ruled the Silk Road," April 16, 2014, http://io9.gizmodo.com/sogdia-the-lost-empire-that-ruled-the-silk-road-1553078058

Rose, Jenny. "The Sogdians: Prime Movers between Boundaries," *Comparative Studies of South Asia, Africa, and the Middle East*, vol. 30, no. 3, 2010.

World and Regional History, Sixth Century

Brown, Peter. *The World of Late Antiquity: AD 150-750* (W.W. Norton & Company, 1989).

Herrin, Judith. *Byzantium: The Surprising Life of a Medieval Empire* (Princeton University Press, 2009).

Hoyland, Robert. *Arabia and the Arabs: From the Bronze Age to the Coming of Islam* (Routledge, 2001).

McKissack, Fredrick et al. *The Royal Kingdoms of Ghana, Mail, and Songhay: Life in Medieval Africa* (Square Fish, 2016).

Phillipson, D.W. *Ancient Ethiopia: Aksum, Its Predecessors and Successors* (British Museum Press, 1998).

Wright, Arthur. *The Sui Dynasty* (Knopf, 1978).

Preview

Silver Screen Sleuths

Curated by Nicole Petit

It's a rollicking Riot of Crime-Solving Fun!
All your favorite stars pull on their deerstalkers and investigate!

Adventurous mysteries in the tradition of old Hollywood

Award-winning curator Nicole Petit presents seven all-new mystery stories featuring the stars of Golden Age Hollywood. Basil Rathbone plays a game of deduction and death against a madman convinced he's as good as Sherlock Holmes. Errol Flynn crosses swords with men who take his star-power a bit too literally.

Ginger Rogers, Lucille Ball, Jimmy Stewart, and Henry Fonda have a double date with murder in the legendary Coconut Grove. Shirley Temple pays a diplomatic visit to West Berlin as plans for a German super-communication device are stolen, and a little girl is caught in the crossfire.

A paranoid director tasks Vincent Price with discovering why a dead man was found in his ancient temple set. George Zucco's latest low-budget western is interrupted by murder—and the ancient cult that may have committed them. Margaret Rutherford tangles with Nazis at a stately manor home where all may not be as it seems.

Silver Screen Sleuths presents mystery stories in the style and tradition of Golden Age B-movie mysteries, starring the stars themselves.

Curated by Nicole Petit and featuring stories by Josh Reynolds, Jon Black, James Bojaciuk, C.L. Werner, M.H. Norris, William Martin, & John Linwood Grant.

A Scandal in Hollywood
Jon Black

Thursday, April 25th

"Honestly, I'm surprised the movies do so well," Basil Rathbone said. "Sherlock Holmes is an anachronism in the age of Raymond Chandler and Dashiell Hammett."

While the reporter from *Motion Picture Magazine* took notes, Basil stirred his coffee as the pair sat in the Universal Studio commissary.

"It sounds as if you don't like Holmes very much?" The journalist, a middle-aged gentleman with a bushy white walrus mustache, had a trace of the Continental in his accent.

That relieved Basil. His English accent often so charmed American reporters that they didn't pay attention to his words. "After shooting on *Dressed to Kill* wraps us week, I will have played Holmes twelve times. Twice for Fox. The rest for Universal. After Playing one character a dozen times, any actor would be ready to move on."

Basil paused, deciding whether to continue. "Counting my stage career, I've played 52 roles from 23 of Shakespeare's plays? My first professional acting job was with the official company at Stratford-on-Avon. I gravitate toward roles with nuance. Even a bit of darkness. I've played Iago, Cassius, Tybalt, Dickens' Murdstone, Pontius Pilate, even Judas Iscariot. Even my screen villains like Sir Guy of Gisbourne in *The Adventures of Robin Hood* had some depth."

"Don't you have anything good to say about Holmes?" The reporter sounded shocked.

A true fan of Sherlock, then. Basil met them often. Though their enthusiasm for the character mystified him, he felt a pang of sympathy accentuated, perhaps, by the band of pale skin around the reporter's finger. An absent ring meant a likely widower. "I will say this," Basil began,

"Sherlock Holmes is unwavering in fighting for good even in danger's face. In that, he is an example to all of us."

The four o'clock interview had been his last task for the day. Leaving the commissary for his studio dressing room, he looked forward to relaxing before driving home. Jane, Basil's personal assistant, intercepted him. "Mina Reeves is here to see you. She had a key to your dressing room so I told her to let herself in," she explained.

Basil often found his assistant's dark eyes difficult to read. This time Jane's expression clearly asked *Did I do right?*

"Very good, Jane." Basil glanced at his pocket watch. "Isn't it time for you to head home? I'll see you tomorrow."

It surprised him that Mina came calling after so many months. True, they'd spent time together last year. But they had drifted. Such things happened. Yet now she warmed his chair. Blonde curls bounced with a will of their own and her curves were precisely as the year 1946 declared they should be. Like many others, she had chased big dreams to Hollywood from the Midwest. But Mina never learned to project her real life beauty onto the screen. So her career languished amidst walk-on parts and bit roles.

Despite efforts at touching up her makeup, she'd clearly been crying "Oh, Baz," she looked at him with despair.

Perhaps it was that tender diminutive, Baz, which got to him. It hadn't passed her lips since they'd grown apart. Feeling unexpectedly protective, Basil knelt beside her. "Mina, what's wrong?"

Suppressing a sob, she handed Basil a cream-colored paper from her purse.

Miss Reeves, I possess photographs of you and a certain Universal Studios actor in a private moment at Arroyo Burro Beach during August of last year. If you do not wish those photographs made public, be at 3627 Mission Road at 10 p.m. this evening and bring your actor friend.

Basil remembered the day. After picnicking, they

slipped further up the beach to a secluded spot. How someone had obtained photos, he didn't understand. But he understood Hollywood's hypocrisy. Photos would barely touch him. They would ruin her. He would help. A gentleman did the right thing and he had been genuinely fond of Mina.

Basil reached for the phone, wanting to tell Ouida he would be home late, before remembering she had was in New York for a screenwriter's conference. That was just as well. Explaining would be complicated. Ouida was the love of his life. And he, hers. But they had an understanding. Neither asked how the other spent private time. Escorting Mina to the Universal Pictures parking lot, they left the studio in his beloved '39 Packard. At the lot's exit, a portly security guard he knew only as "Chester" gave a friendly wave. But Basil was not unaware of the slight tightening around the corner of the Chester's eyes, as if to say "Oh, are you two together again?" Inwardly, Basil sighed. Studios were like giant small towns. Negotiating through the tight Universal City streets, Basil nudged the Packard onto the highway.

Though the twilight, the lights on the HOLLYWOODLAND sign already twinkled in the distance. It took 4,000 bulbs to illuminate the 13 white letters atop Mount Lee, each over 50 feet tall, flashing, in turn:

HOLLY   WOOD   LAND

A dispute over the sign's electric bill raged between the city and the developer who originally erected the sign. Many suspected the landmark would soon go dark. Basil had no feelings either way.

Though hours remained until their mysterious appointment, Basil's foot pressed heavily on the Packard's gas pedal. He loved speed, but tonight it was speed with a purpose. He wanted to reach his bank before it closed. Everything pointed toward blackmail. But no dollar amount or other demands had been given. Either they were dealing with an amateur or something stranger was afoot. Both possibilities unnerved Basil.

It would be lying to say he had no concerns for himself. Or for Ouida. But Mina was the one in real professional, and personal, jeopardy. Knowing how the system worked, he cringed. It wasn't having the affair that would ruin Mina. It was the getting caught.

There were, of course, means for procuring cash after banking hours. But, reflecting that they increased risk of the very publicity he wished to avoid, Basil rode his accelerator even harder.

With minutes to spare, he sloppily double-parked the Packard at the bank's entrance. Normally, such a parking job would have driven him to distraction but time was of the essence. Already halfway out the door, he turned back to Mina. "Will you be alright waiting here?"

She nodded. Striding toward the bank, he heard her whisper after him "Thank you, Baz."

Five minutes later he was back in the car. In absence of specific instructions from their blackmailer, he had discretely withdrawn funds sufficient to cover any price the maligner would likely ask.

Basil drove southeast through the deepening dusk. As natural illumination dimmed, the city's million electric lights winked to life. Looking around, it was difficult to believe that the world had been in flames just a year ago. Sure, this city experienced some war nerves in those dark, final days of 1941. And, throughout the duration, L.A. had been America's great arsenal. Of airplanes. Of vehicles. And of morale, Hollywood had gone to war, too. But L.A. never looked back.

Like magic, new ribbons of concrete highways, and legions of speeding new cars to fill them, spilled across the map. At every off-ramp, new neighborhoods swelled with returned GIs and their young families. With much of the world still in recovery, Basil found something unseemly yet alluring about it all. The future was being made in L.A. And it fell to Hollywood to properly instruct the rest of the world about what the future looked like.

Finding the silence uncomfortable, Basil asked Mina how she'd been keeping busy.

Her last screen role had been *Girl on the Spot,* a crime drama mixed with a musical which Universal released, amid not much fanfare, earlier in the year. From the beginning, Basil had been skeptical about its dubious mix of genres. Mina relayed how, after being signed for a small chorus role, she had been bumped down to a non-speaking extra. Until she landed another film role, she was keeping body and soul together with catalogue modeling; her most notable coup as a swimwear model for Broadway Department Store.

Basil suggested she audition for *Little Miss Big.* The upcoming frothy, family-friendly comedy would play to Mina's strengths. As would its director, Erle Kenton. The Missourian was known to have penchant for hiring supporting actors who shared his middle-of-the-country origins. Knowing a little of the man, Basil offered Mina some suggestions for getting on Kenton's good side.

After their awkward discussion of Mina's modest successes, she visibly relaxed while talking about her family in Illinois. But, after running out of things to say to about her parents, the grocery they owned, and her eight brothers and sisters, she lapsed back into silence. For lack of anything else to say, Basil shared his feeling about leaving *Dressed to Kill*, and Sherlock Holmes, behind.

"I will miss Nigel Bruce," he confided, regarding the Scotsman who had been his Watson through all 14 Holmes pictures. As a light went on in his mind, Basil slapped the steering wheel. "That's something I should have told the reporter. He would have appreciated it." Basil recounted his interview with the *Motion Picture Magazine* reporter. "As wooden as Doyle's writing can be," he expounded to Mina "the interplay between Holmes and Watson always had real life. Real feeling. That's hard to do. It's a very tricky chemistry. You might think you have it when you don't. Or, when you're not expecting it at all, suddenly it's there."

Basil showed more enthusiasm discussing his previous film, *Heartbeat*. "I played Professor Aristide, a Fagin-esque character operating a school for pickpockets in Paris." He could hardly blame Mina for showing greater interest in Ginger Rogers, who played the film's ingénue protagonist, than Basil's role as her foil. Still, in defense of his pride, he added "Though hardly high art, at least Professor Aristide was role with some meat on it!"

With his thoughts brought back to Sherlock Holmes, Basil made a candid admission, "Mina, I fear Holmes will cast a long shadow over me. He is someone I must not and will not play again regardless of circumstance."

Though Basil had not recognized the addresses 3627 Mission Road, in the Lincoln Heights neighborhood, he instantly recognized the destination: the Los Angeles Alligator Farm. Ostensibly an aquaculture business with an educational sideline, everyone in L.A. knew what the alligator farm really was. A tourist trap.

Finding its parking lot empty, Basil wondered if their man might be more professional than he had thought. At least he avoided the amateurish mistake of making his means of transportation obvious…and allowing his victims to note his car's make and model. Taking the lead into an unknown and possibly dangerous situation, Basil felt like thirty years had fallen away and he was once again leading patrols in the Great War.

Approaching the alligator farm's white faux-Greek

Revival main building and gift shop, they passed signs proclaiming "Over 1,000 Alligators" and "See the Trained Alligator Show" intermixed with paintings of strapping young men and buxom young women wrestling the creatures.

Finding its front doors locked, Basil peered through the building's windows. The darkened interior appeared depopulated. Whomever they were meeting wasn't inside. Making their way around the farm's outer wall, Basil discovered a side gate left ajar…a gate leading directly into the open area containing the farm's toothsome exhibits. The gate creaked. Mina jumped as Basil pushed it open.

Tensely, they searched the immediate area for their blackmailer. "Please tell me you have some funny story about being in a movie with an alligator to take my mind off this," Mina said hopefully.

"Me personally? No." As Basil responded, he began purposefully scanning the area near the main entrance until he found a circular tank occupied by a single, massive alligator. "Billy" proclaimed a sign at the tank's edge. "But I'll bet this fellow could tell you a story or two. Would you believe I'm jealous of this reptile?"

"Why?" asked Mina, perplexed.

"Because he's been in more movies than I have. Almost any time you see an alligator or supposed crocodile on the big screen: jungle movies, swamp movies, horror movies, it's been played by Billy here."

The reptile regarded the pair with lazy indifference. Not too different, Basil thought drolly, from what most other big Hollywood stars would give their fans. "I hear he's even trained. After a fashion. Dangling a bit of meat above him, just off camera, he always opens wide. You would expect other alligators to do the same. Apparently they don't. Supposedly, he even lets his trainer ride around on his back. I don't suggest we put that to the test."

Fascinating as it was to meet the world's most famous

reptile, Billy wasn't why they were here. But they had yet
to find any sign of the person who had summoned them.
Apparently, Basil and Mina were expected to work for the
privilege of being blackmailed.

They picked their way along paths winding past
concrete ponds and through replica bayous hung with faux
Spanish moss as they sought their mysterious host.
Deserted and dark, the alligator farm possessed a surreal,
almost nightmarish quality. Shadowy shapes floating in the
water remained so silent and still it was difficult to believe
they were alive. Occasionally, one became agitated,
splashing furiously about while uttering their distinctive
primordial bellow. Basil couldn't say whether the statue-
like stillness or the sudden bursts of frenzied activity
unnerved him more. As Mina reached forward to take his
hand in hers, Basil expected he felt as comforted as she did.

"I've been thinking," he said as they crossed a narrow
causeway between two reptile-infested ponds "If this places
operates without its attractions eating its visitors on a
regular basis, they must keep their animals gorged to the
point of gluttony. I suspect our danger is actually minimal."
Basil knew his reasoning was entirely sound. He didn't
know who he was trying to convince. Mina? Or himself?

His fondness for animals did not extend to the beasts
surrounding them. And had not since he was very young.
Involuntarily, against his better judgement in fact, Basil
shared a story. "I think I told you that I was born in South
Africa? We lived there until I was three, when the local
Boers started suspecting my father was a British agent and
we had to flee on short notice.

"One of my last memories of Africa was a country
outing with my parents. While picnicking by a stream, a
reedbuck appeared. I don't know if you've seen a reedbuck,
Mina. It's an antelope. With elegant, inward curving horns
and beautiful, nearly human eyes. Normally they're quite
skittish. But this one, after taking our measure for a few

moments, walked confidently past us to drink. For a child, there was something magical in that moment. But, mid-drink, a crocodile shot from the stream, took the reedbuck's neck in its jaws, and dragged it into the water where several its fellows appeared and joined in tearing the poor animal to pieces."

"Thanks, Baz. I feel so much better now," she replied with sarcasm so thick that even the alligators could have detected it.

"Sorry," Basil replied, slightly embarrassed. "It's just such a vivid memory. It made quite an impression on me. For whatever it may be worth, I've heard alligators are not as aggressive as crocodiles."

In the end, it was Mina who spotted the Manila envelope taped to the property's rear wall. Opening it, Basil discovered the photographs and negatives, accompanied by another letter. To his surprise, the missive was written in Greek. As a young man at Repton School, he'd studied the language. Basil was the first to admit he had not been a diligent student and, anyway, that was 40 years ago. Still, he could fumble his way along.

> *Dear Mister Rathbone,*
> *I hope finding a Greek Interpreter has not taken overlong. Thank you for coming. Please excuse this theatrical means of getting your attention. You have the once in a lifetime opportunity to play your greatest role ... in reality. Unless you stop me, at sunset next Friday I will unleash calamity upon your city. Please do not go to the police or otherwise publicize this matter. Otherwise, I shall be forced to move up my timetable or take other drastic action.*

Preview

Midnight

By M.H. Norris

Dr. Rosella Tassoni is not a ghost hunter. She is not a traditional forensic anthropologist either. Her goal is to solve the crime hiding behind various myths, legends, ghost stories, and internet games gone wrong.

Taking a chance and deciding to go into business for herself, Rosella finds herself on a case that could make or break her career before it has a chance to start. Will she find herself in over her head?

All The Petty Myths is an anthology that features the first mystery featuring Forensic Mythologist Dr. Rosella Tassoni. This collection also features stories from Marc Sorondo, James Bojaciuk, and D.J. Tyre.

DR. ROSELLA TASSONI looked over the auditorium full of half-asleep freshman and quickly remembered why she *usually* only agreed to lecture upper-level courses.

"Since the beginning of time, man has told stories. When a written language came along, these were written down. Some would surpass their own cultures, becoming what we know to be legends. Today we call the study of those legends mythology. Every culture has their own distinct legends, yet many share a similar foundation. Max Müller considered these legends 'a disease of language,' but clearly they're something more. I prefer Tolkien's explanation for legends in his essay 'On Fairy-Stories,' originally delivered to students very similar to you. 'The history of fairy-stories is probably more complex than the physical history of the human race, and as complex as the history of human language.'"

Rosella clicked the slide over before reading the quote. "What are the origins of, as Tolkien would call them, 'fairy-stories'? 'I am too unlearned to deal with this question in any other way than with a few remarks…It is plain enough that fairy-stories (in wider or in narrower sense) are very ancient indeed. Related things appear in very early records; and they are found universally, wherever there is language. We are therefore obviously confronted with a variant of the problem that the archaeologist encounters, or the comparative philologist: with the debate between independent evolution (or rather invention) of the similar; inheritance from a common ancestry; and diffusion at various times from one or more centres."

Turning away from the screen she studied the crowd. "Tolkien is considered one of the greatest fantasy writers in the history of mankind. His books are still widely read and have even inspired a popular MMORPG."

That comment helped her pick out the gamers in the audience by their grins. She could tell a couple of them were thinking about playing that as soon as class was over. In fact, the way one boy's head shot up, she couldn't help but wonder if she looked at his screen if she would find Middle-Earth.

"But, more than that, he was one of the great philologists, with an intense knowledge of language's history—and the mythology that has always clung to it. *Gilgamesh*, after all, is our earliest surviving written record. Tolkien acknowledged Müller's quote though and had this to say, 'Max Müller's view of mythology as a 'disease of language' can be abandoned without regret. Mythology is not a disease at all, though it may, like all human things, become diseased. You might as well say that thinking is a disease of the mind. It would be more near the truth to say that languages, especially modern European languages, are a disease of mythology.'"

That caused her to chuckle. "I prefer to agree with Tolkien on this. After all, that quote is how I earn my living, in a sense."

As she walked across the stage, clicking through slides, she eyed one of the students. He slipped into the back of the lecture hall, border-lining the time that it was socially acceptable to arrive late. Which was, also, the time it was polite for Rosella to be late. She'd earned her doctorate. At least according to the old myth—Rosella preferred to be on time to speaking events, not in the mood to waste not only her time but the time of those listening. The student quickly opened his laptop and tried to look attentive, but his shoulders were tense yet his face portrayed a different story. His face appeared to be relaxed but his clenched jaw told her he was stressed and a little over focused on the task at hand. Not only that but she could see his wire from here. He must be new, he was too tense. That or he hadn't been warned that she was pretty good at reading body language. But seriously, Quantico was slipping if they thought that act was covert. She assumed he was wired simply to test him in the field, in a safe situation. Baby's first op.

"Some stories are to teach a lesson, it's the reason we have fables and how Aesop became a household name. Others are fun stories to tell around a campfire or a childhood sleepover or to be turned into the next Disney movie."

"Others take a darker side, or rather people choose to let them." Another click another slide.

"Serial killers, immortalized in this day and age by the influx of crime dramas which seem to occupy most major networks. People are obsessed with the idea of the forensic sciences."

Now she had their attention.

"Sometimes, the two meet. Killers think they can hide behind the myths. Forensic Mythology if you will."

A student in the fourth row raised her hand and Rosella nodded to her. Being called on by a guest would at least give her a good story. She was one of the ones who'd perked up at the mention of *Lord of the Rings Online*. Her Mac was plastered with stickers—a TARDIS design that went out with the sixties, a *Metropolitan* press badge reading Smith, and Mara Jade holding a pink lightsaber aloft; it was clear this girl knew her science fiction and fantasy. Her straight posture and over-eager expression let Rosella know that this was probably one of her friend's better students.

"So, you're saying that most urban myths aren't true?"

Rosella smiled. "That's not my job to figure out; that was more something Margaret McConnell studied to learn, and I direct you to her books. I prefer to leave that to other people to argue over. I have to sort the very real killer from the myth."

Another hand, this time from a boy who had looked bored until she had said "serial killers." Then his attitude changed rather quickly and the combination of that, along with the book by Temperance Brennan in his bag, made her wonder if he knew how much was real and how much was fiction. Though at least he was reading one of the more accurate adaptations. Nodding to him, she was partially curious what question he'd come up with.

"How do the two manage to come together? Mythology's just stories. Forensic Science is an actual science."

It was a question she often got. With a nod she clicked a slide. "Most people wonder how I manage to see the two combined. Who here has gotten one of those annoying chain emails, the ones that say if you don't pass it on you'll bad luck or meet an untimely demise?"

Hands all over the auditorium went up. They usually did when she asked the question.

"A few years ago in Dallas, Texas one of those went around. The thing was, people who didn't pass it along met said untimely demise."

She clicked a slide and showed a set of three victims. Each one had received a single bullet wound. A tarot baring the reverse chariot was laid beside them. "All of our victims had received that email within twenty-four hours of their death and for a while that was our only tie-in. Forensic science—the wound delivered at point blank, the presence of the card. Fornensic mythology—the email, and the card itself. When reversed, the chariot tarot card means bad luck."

"Did you catch the guy?" Someone near the back asked without raising their hand.

"Eventually. He managed to kill five victims before we were able to nail down his location. But when killers use something like these superstitious emails or urban legends, they often use them as a mask to hide their crimes. Some people are so focused on the legend coming true that they refuse to see what's right in front of them—a human being."

"So the myths aren't true?" The over-eager girl repeated her earlier question.

"Once again, I didn't say that. It's not my business to prove or disprove them. Though I will say those annoying emails are probably the creation of someone who had too much time on their hands and more than enough access to the internet."

That earned her a few chuckles. "Forensic Mythology is an emerging sub-classification of the forensic sciences. And while many of my colleagues don't think it's practical, I do know that it has helped to save lives and bring peace to victims."

Another hand went up and she nodded to the person about halfway back. "But why mythology? What made you think to combine it with the forensic sciences?"

Rosella launched into her traditional lecture, smiling at how once again, she had managed to get the students to steer the conversation to where she wanted to go. Of course, they didn't realize that that's what just happened.

The rest of the class passed quickly and soon enough students were packing up to rush off to their next class, a hot date, a procrastinated study session, or one of the seemingly endless things students could do. Finally, the tardy student from earlier made his way up, carrying a copy of her latest book in his hand.

"You know, you can drop the cover now. A tip, when your body language sends mixed signals, a trained eye is going to notice."

The kid's face dropped and he shrugged. "They said you were good. Does that mean you won't sign my book? I actually really enjoyed it."

Rosella let out a chuckle. "I'll sign it. I'm assuming somewhere in that bag there's a file for me?"

"A case came up and my superior wanted you to take a look. He thinks it might be up your alley."

"Your superior knows that, officially, I'm not here." Rosella let out a sigh, the extremely long to-do list she had made for this trip to DC suddenly seeming unattainable.

"According to him, it's right up your alley Also, he said something about covering your hotel here and rescheduling any appointments you miss to take a look."

She turned to Professor Alicia Walter, an old friend of hers. "I might have to take a raincheck on that coffee."

A LARGE CAN OF SALT—the brand gave away that it had been bought at the local dollar store—sat beside a pillar candle in a glass drawer. It was probably of the same origin of its twin, which tipped over beside a taped silhouette. It gave Rosella a hint of the sad story that had played out here, a couple of days ago.

Rosella rubbed over a bloodstain with a gloved hand and didn't try to hold in a sigh.

"I don't get it." She turned to see the Sheriff Kristopher Peake studying her studying the scene. "I've seen it so many times and I still don't get it."

She pulled the case file out of her bag and looked at the picture of fifteen-year-old Ashley Coats. Honor Roll, freshman at Huntington Prep, involved with the SGA. A fairly large amount of friends on Facebook, a couple hundred followers on Twitter. Nothing indicated that something like this could happen to her.

But that silhouette proved otherwise.

Five kids, five crime scenes, all within just a few hours of each other on a Friday night. The salt and the candle gave away that it was a ritual of some kind. What had Ashley gotten into?

She grabbed the file again as she heard someone enter the room.

"Who is she?" a voice asked the Sheriff.

"Someone the FBI called in. Apparently, she's an expert on cases like this."

"And we weren't consulted?"

"We have jurisdiction here."

Rosella looked at the photos of the crime scene and noticed that Ashley was cut open, hence the large blood stain on the floor. "And we have a group of dead kids and no evidence that this *isn't* going to happen again so if you are going to act like small children can you at least do it outside and let me work? Thank you."

She wandered into the kitchen, mentally ticking off different cultures, different rituals, but it was always a mix of what was and what wasn't there. She opened the cabinets until she found the spices. Garlic, oregano, cilantro—nothing outside the usual household collection. Shutting the cabinets, she walked around the kitchen peeking in the pantry.

198

"All the internal organs were missing when the coroner came, right?" She walked past the group of law enforcement officers to the other side of the house. "From all of the victims?"

"Wasn't a pretty sight."

Rosella nodded as she continued to wander the house. Matches littered the floor in a couple of places. Looking at the notes, she searched for the time of death. The coroner estimated it to be around three in the morning. She added discussing a few things with him to her mental to-do list.

That time of death did narrow down the ritual some more.

She wandered into the bathroom, peeking in the drawers and cabinets. But nothing in Ashley's bathroom showed anything outside of the ordinary for a girl her age.

The parents' room was first, but looked basically untouched. "Where are her parents?"

"Staying with some friends until after the funeral on Wednesday," an officer who had been bagging something in Ashley's room answered.

"Have they been here since?"

"Briefly."

Rosella peeked inside the mother's closet, the faint hint of designer perfume lingering on her clothes. The closet was all women's clothes; the husband's must have been in a guest room. There was another match off to the side of the master bathroom floor.

She made her way into the girl's room, not surprised at the hottie-of-the-month's face all over her walls. CDs took a shelf where books should be, and her laptop sat on her bed. With a groan, she saw all ten seasons of *Supernatural*. Of course she watched that show. Victims in Rosella's line always seemed to. Next to it sat a couple of seasons of *American Duos* and Rosella quickly shoved away the nagging feeling that she'd forgotten to TiVo it.

Right now, she needed to focus.

As she crossed the threshold, she looked down and saw a piece of paper. In flowing script was Ashley's name and a drop of blood.

That *really* narrowed it down.

Rosella knocked on the door three times. Wood.

There were a couple more matches by the door.

"Make sure you bag up the matches we're finding all over the floor."

Coming into the room, she looked under the bed, between the mattress and the pad, between books, and in the drawers. Besides the things at the door, this room could have belonged to any teenager.

"What's the verdict?"

Rosella turned to see the Sheriff leaning up against the doorframe of the parent's room.

"Sometimes, when figuring out what ritual, it's a mix of what's there or what's not there."

"A ritual?" The Sheriff looked troubled. "What do you mean?"

"The salt, the candles, it was a ritual. There were several options that would require both of those. Actually, most preternatural related, modern rituals require both."

"Preternatural, don't you mean supernatural?"

Rosella crossed her arms as she felt her eyebrow reach for her hairline. "Would people stop misusing that term? This was a *preternatural* ritual."

Seeing the blank look on his face—she sighed, and slipped into lecture mode. "Preternatural is used to refer to actions that are demonic in nature. Supernatural refers to acts of God. The word is often bastardized into meaning 'things beyond nature.'"

"You're saying she was practicing witchcraft?"

"I am not."

"Summing this up, demons had something to do with this? But she didn't practice witchcraft."

Staring the man down, she decided to cut him a break, for now. "Ashley here unknowingly engaged into a preternatural ritual. In fact, I'm fairly certain I know which one it is."

"What is it?"

Rosella made her way back into the family room where the silhouette still sat on the floor. "It looks like she summoned the Midnight Man. And he won the game."

Preview

The Mouth of the Ness

By William Meikle

The first novella in Josh Reynolds and James Bojaciuk's series *Cryptid Clash!*, William Meikle's The Mouth of the Ness shows us what emerges from the Wyrd when Vikings go a-raiding.

TOR TORSSON STOOD at the dragon's head as the longboat made its way by oar up a foggy firth. They were reaching shallower shoals but his concern was not with possible obstacles in the water, but with his friend, Skald Orjan who sat on the deck rolling the bones and muttering to himself. The seer had been lost in the Wyrd all morning, and the rest of the Viking crew were starting to mutter, seeing the crippled mystic's behavior as an ill omen for the raid to come.

"What do you see, Orjan?" he asked. To Tor the youth at his feet would always be Orjan Persson, the boy who'd almost died in a rock fall and his lifelong friend, not the crippled youth who fought like a Berserker and spoke to the Fates that the other men saw. But neither facet of the Skald was talking—he just kept muttering, almost under his breath. One of the words was 'doom', but Tor wasn't about to relay that to the rest of the Vikings—not on his first sail as Captain.

Besides, it was the Skald's vision in the Wyrd that had brought them this far. The Scottish highland capital, Inverness, was somewhere in the fog ahead. Skald had seen it in a vision, even while sitting by the fjord at home—the town and, beyond that at the head of a long inland fjord, an abbey that hoarded great wealth of gold, silver. There was more—a secret that Orjan could not see, but knew was worth a King's ransom could it be taken; a worthy prize for a Viking raid.

It hadn't taken Tor long after Skald told him of the abbey to persuade his uncle to let him undertake the journey—both Tor and the Skald had more than earned the right on their last trip out. There, in the wild arctic lands to the east of Sweden, the Skald had discovered the true depths of his tie to the Wyrd, and Tor had saved a whole crew with his strength, courage and wits.

Now here they were, approaching Scotland after two weeks at sea, Captain and Seer, brothers in blood and glory, with a prize in their sights. The trip itself had been uneventful, but the closer they got to the Scottish shores, the more Skald retreated into himself, called into the misty dreams of the Wyrd and travels in the mystic—places where Tor could not accompany him. This time he had been gone for several hours, and Tor was starting to consider a forcible awakening when Skald finally looked up from the bones and nodded.

Tor hefted his sword—a last gift from Ragnar before their departure, and tapped twice on the dragon's head. It was done softly, and would be heard no more than ten yards away in the fog, but the sound echoed enough in the long timbers that the crew took heed and stopped rowing. The longboat drifted inside a flat calm in thick fog, trusting to the Skald's sight that they were close enough to Inverness to need caution from here on. Tor had never been given cause to doubt his friend's counsel—and had it confirmed yet again when they heard the sound of a church bell toll in the fog—a matter of several hundred yards away at most.

They had come across the expanse of the Northern Sea, and were now as close they could get to the highland capital without being noticed. Now they must do little but wait for nightfall, and their chance to creep through the strait at Inverness and into the loch of the Ness, where the prize awaited them.

They broke bread and had some ale, still drifting in the fog. The crew was in fine spirits despite having rowed for several hours against the current. As ever, they were respectful of Skald when he was close to their captain, but Tor saw many give his friend the sign of the evil eye as he passed toward the rear of the boat where he liked to eat— alone. Tor sighed inwardly—if he could give his friend peace, he would, at any price that might be demanded—but there was little sign of peace or rest in either of their immediate futures, and he forced his thoughts back to the task at hand as the fog darkened around them. Somewhere beyond the mist, night was falling—and the Viking was about to begin properly. Despite his worry for the Skald, Tor felt his excitement rise and his grip tightened on his newly gifted sword.

There was fortune and glory ahead of them—and he meant to take as much of both as was to be had.

THE SKALD CAME FORWARD again as a breeze came up and the fog cleared to show the last of the sun going down beyond a town ahead of them, where the north and south shores converged.

"The strait is narrow—but there will be no moon," he said. "Our passage should be simple enough if we are quiet."

"You have seen this?" Tor asked, and for the first time in days the Skald laughed.

"Yes—I looked up," he said, then winced and clutched his leg. The damp always pained the old wound, and at times Tor wished it had been he, not Orjan that had been pinned under that rock, if only to spare the hurt he knew his friend suffered. But the Skald waved Tor away when he expressed concern.

"It is no worse—and no better—than it has ever been. And it will be that way until I go to the Wyrd for the last time, so there is no use in me complaining. Come—let us see if we can get beyond the town—I will get an hour and more of rest once we are on the loch itself."

The two of them stood at the prow as the twenty-four oarsmen—all well practiced in silent rowing, took them slowly toward the town, whose firelights were now showing red against the darkening night.

They kept to the south side of the channel—the shoreline there was densely wooded and looked to be uninhabited, and they crept as close to the tree line as was safe in the dark so that their silhouette would not be seen against the sky. Tor held his breath as they past within arrow distance of the keep on the hill that stood guard over Inverness township, but there were no warning cries; no fires were lit. Within minutes they had left the town behind. Ten minutes after that the strait widened to more of an open river—it was tidal at this point and, as they had come in on the rising current of the night tide, they negotiated the shallows with ease. Five minutes after that the longboat emerged into the wide breadth of the loch itself and they were able to unfurl the sail as an easterly breeze got up at their back. The sailcloth snapped in the wind and the longboat bucked, once, then started to make good time under sail along the length of the loch.

"How far?" Tor asked.

"It is on the north bank—a couple of hours sail in calm waters, which is good news for our chances of success, as the later we arrive, the less prepared they will be for an attack."

"It does not matter how prepared they are," Tor said with a grim smile. "You say they are monks? I have never heard of any man of the cloth prepared to stand against a Viking raid—I doubt these Scots are any different to their counterparts in the South."

But Tor was not about to abandon all subtlety or caution. He placed a man on watch on either side of the prow—there were only scattered settlements along the loch side, rarely more than two or three fires in each one and a mile or more between each one. But he preferred to err on the side of caution—at least until the prize was in sight.

Skald went back to sitting on the deck just behind the dragon's head, his bad leg outstretched, straight in front of him like a bit of dead wood. He called Tor down to join him, putting his head close so that no one would overhear.

"We have talked of the prize, you and I—but we have not talked of the hidden secret—and now I believe we must, for I have seen further into the Wyrd on my most recent sojourn there—we are sailing into trouble."

It was Tor's turn to laugh.

"We are Viking. We are always sailing into trouble."

Skald did not smile in return.

"There is indeed a prize ahead—but there is also darkness there—a writhing, smothering, monstrous darkness. It hangs over the abbey like a great serpent, barring all my attempts to see past it."

Tor did not much like the direction the conversation was taking.

"Was it not you that showed us this prize in the first place? You said it was a great thing—a wonder that would make our names as Vikings. Do not say we should turn away now."

Skald spoke even more quietly, scarcely more than a whisper.

"I merely propose caution…"

Tor laughed again, and repeated his earlier words.

"What need have we for a surfeit of caution—we are Viking. We will take that abbey, have their secret, and be on the way home with the outgoing tide in the morning. Take heart, Orjan; great deeds await us. They will sing about us in song in ages yet to come."

Tor saw Skald decide to keep quiet—he knew that look of old—a desire not to annoy a friend. But if there really was dark danger ahead, Tor had to know, for the sake of his crew.

"Tell me," he said. "Tell me what you are not saying. And if it makes you feel better about it—your captain commands you to speak."

That did get him a smile.

"Since when has that ever worked with me? But you are right—as Captain here, you need to know—but I fear you might not understand, for it is a thing of the Wyrd."

"You mean it is something of the Gods—something from Asgard itself?"

"It is certainly of the mist—and more of Niflheim than Asgard. Whatever it is, it is strong, it is fearsome—and it protects the secret of the Abbey. Perhaps we might be content with the gold and silver? For this other thing—it is beyond my ken—beyond anything I want to ken."

Tor saw the worry in his friend's face, and clapped Skald on the shoulder.

"I will take whatever counsel you offer, my friend. If the abbey coffers have sufficient gold and silver, then we will have that, and that alone. It will surely be enough—I too have no wish to meddle further in the ways of the Wyrd—certainly not this far from hearth and home."

Skald fell quiet again, and Tor left him to his thoughts. He stood at the dragon's head watching the shores as the longboat glided, almost silently, up the long, wide, loch under a dark, cloud-covered sky. Once again he felt excitement rise at the prospect ahead. It was well known among the Norsemen that most of the White Christ's abbeys held wealth. It seemed to Tor that the Mediterranean god was more interested in raising taxes and accruing wealth than any religion had a right to be, but if it meant more plunder for him and his people, he was not going to pass it by. Especially as this particular abbey, thought too remote and too far from the sea to be in danger, was so little defended—and so easily accessible with only a modicum of stealth.

He stood there for several hours, the only sound the snap of wind in the said and the soft lapping of wavelets on the prow. He drifted into a watchful state he'd learned on long nights on guard on his home shores—somewhere between dozing and wakefulness where his eyes saw but his mind wandered, only coming alert at anything untoward in his field of vision.

Finally, some two hours after making sail, Tor gripped his sword hilt tighter as a darker shadow showed against the night sky on the north shore ahead of them. They had reached their destination.

He tapped lightly on the decks with the sword—twice—and the crew got the message. They dropped the sail. The steersman at the rudder—with the aid of the slight breeze—brought the longboat in a silent drift ever closer to the shore.

The abbey was built atop a rocky outcrop that jutted into the lock from the north shore. There were no defenses visible, and no windows showed any light—it was merely a dark block of stone with a tall tower at one end, although the walls were high and thick, and there a single iron gate on the south side to mark the only entrance.

"Caution, Tor," Skald said—but the young captain's blood was up at the thought of glory. The anchor was dropped, and Tor leapt out of the boat even before it hit bottom, splashing through thigh deep water toward the dark shore. The rest of the crew followed—even Skald, who Tor had wanted to stay in the longboat, but who insisted on joining the attack.

He waited on the shingle shore until the crew was all disembarked. He did not need to discuss tactics—each man knew his job and knew the goal. He showed them his sword, pointed it at the abbey, and as a man they moved quickly off the small beach onto the approach to the building itself.

There was no defense mounted—the gate was not even locked—it creaked open at a single push and within seconds the party of Vikings were inside the abbey itself. At first Tor thought that their arrival had been anticipated and that the abbey had been emptied, far all seemed dark, quiet and silent. Then he spotted the flicker of candlelight against two tall windows. On investigation they found two dozen monks in the chapel—all praying, none of them armed or inclined to put up any fight. Tor left four men watching them, then scoured the rest of the building.

Skald had been right. They found a small fortune of gold and silver plate in an anteroom of the chapel, an underground storeroom filled with barrels of mead and ale, and even a heavy wooden chest full of a variety of different coinages, much of it in Spanish gold.

There had still been no attempt to stop them as the Vikings lugged their spoils up into the main part of the building. Tor was about to declare the raid a success and head back to the longboat with the plunder when Skald put a hand on his arm.

"There is the other matter—it is in the tall tower overlooking the loch. I can feel it draw at me. Whatever it is, it is strong in the Wyrd—stronger than anything I have ever felt."

"Do you still counsel that we leave it alone?"

Skald shook his head.

"I know not—but now that I am here, I fear having whatever it is at out backs on the return sail. It might be best to have done with it now, while we can. But it should just be we two—the other men would not understand. And it might be perilous."

Tor nodded. He ordered the crew to get their spoils back to the longboat, and with Skald at his side and his sword in his hand, they headed for the tower.

Did you enjoy What You just Read?

If you enjoyed this book, *please* review it on Amazon and GoodReads!

It's the best way to support the author.

For fantastic fiction, in-depth articles by your favourite authors, open submissions, and more, please...

Visit Our Website
18thwall.com/

Like Us on Facebook
facebook.com/18thwall/

Follow Us on Twitter
@18thWall

We'd love to hear from you! You help make these books possible.

www.ingramcontent.com/pod-product-compliance
Lightning Source LLC
Chambersburg PA
CBHW070926250626
47159CB00009B/3135